KV-577-284

THE
SHOCKING
PRICE
OF
A PAIR OF
SHOES

ANDY TILLEY

The Book Guild Ltd

LOUTH
LIBRARY SERVICE

Acc No

Class No

Invoice No

Catalogued   6/10/22

Vendor

First published in Great Britain in 2022 by
The Book Guild Ltd
Unit E2, Airfield Business Park
Harrison Road
Market Harborough
Leicestershire, LE16 7UL
Freephone: 0800 999 2982
www.bookguild.co.uk
Email: info@bookguild.co.uk
Twitter: @bookguild

Copyright © 2022 Andy Tilley

The right of Andy Tilley to be identified as the author of this
work has been asserted by him in accordance with the
Copyright, Design and Patents Act 1988.

All rights reserved. No part of this publication may be
reproduced, transmitted, or stored in a retrieval system, in any form or by any means,
without permission in writing from the publisher, nor be otherwise circulated in
any form of binding or cover other than that in which it is published and without
a similar condition being imposed on the subsequent purchaser.

Typeset in 11pt Adobe Garamond Pro

Printed on FSC accredited paper
Printed and bound in Great Britain by 4edge Limited

ISBN 978 1914471 353

British Library Cataloguing in Publication Data.
A catalogue record for this book is available from the British Library.

For Dad.

Huge thanks to Zane for keeping the characters
true to themselves and the dogs busy.

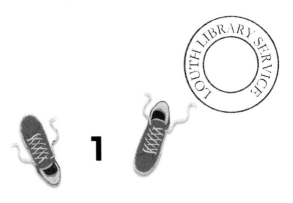

LOUTH LIBRARY SERVICE

1

We all have a dark side. Okay, maybe 'dark' is a bit strong and I'm certainly not claiming that we're all walking around secretly seething and fighting an urge to be evil or cruel – far from it. What I am saying though is this: sometimes generally good people do stuff that they'd rather others didn't know about.

The problem is that being so fundamentally flawed is not an easy thing to accept and so most of us put a lot of effort into either justifying why we made a bad choice or just flat out denying that we even have a dark side at all. But not me: I'm okay with it. I'm happy to look in the mirror and say, *Okay, Liam Slater, at best you're a wannabe good guy who probably falls short from time to time, but nevertheless, you are a net contributor to the world being if not better then certainly more tolerable.*

For example, I'll often smile and invite someone to jump in front of me at the checkout queue, but will I then cross the car park to help them load their shopping into the car? Of course not! I've done my good deed for the day, so instead I'll sling my bags onto the back seat, abandon the shopping trolley and then drive past them, possibly beeping and throwing a finger if their half-full trolley dares to stick out even slightly, forcing me to adjust my steering wheel. I have and know my limits, just as I do occasionally give a few quid to charity, but only when I'm flush. No real sacrifice involved, and I certainly wouldn't get out of bed to go and help out at the local food bank on a Saturday morning. Such are the limits of my goodness, and I'm both familiar and comfy with them. I am, on balance, more light than dark and not the slightest bit shady, and so this is why my landlord's attitude is really winding me up. She's basically accusing me of a wilful, nasty act, making me out to be a slacker and a generally bad person, and it's not fair.

To begin with Barbara's calm and professional manner had given me hope that she knows this not to be the case. Hope that today we would finally resolve our differences amicably and that, after almost three weeks of trying, I'd manage to convince her how serious my situation is. Hope's gone now, though, because as calm as I am with my explanation, repeating it for a third time has apparently really pissed her off. She is suddenly blazing, screaming so loudly that I can feel the venom in her threat even though I've left the phone on the worktop to go and peek out of the kitchen window.

'Listen, Mr Slater, and listen good! Either you or Mr Kelly come to the office today and settle up or this is going to get very nasty very quickly. Understand?'

I do understand. She's telling me that she'll send Barry round if the rent isn't paid, but what she doesn't understand is that I'm not bothered if she does. Oh, there's no doubt that Barry is very big and very scary, but the truth about Barry the Bailiff is that he isn't the enforcer that his mother believes him to be. How do I know this? Eight months of undercover work, that's how. When me and John had first moved to Didsbury we'd taken bar jobs at a small, grubby little back street boozer three doors down from MyPad, Barbara's student accommodation rental business. A local pub for local people, the Red Lion is tiny and really old school: six bar stools and five booths (barely covered by threadbare velour) where people sit to sup Robinson's bitter or one of two draft lagers. The only sign of any interest in upkeep from the landlord over the last ten years is a glass-fronted fridge that sits next to the till. In it Geoff keeps orange juice and Coke for the drivers, but tucked away behind these is something that tells you everything you need to know about his clientele. Six tins of Red Bull tins that are starting to rust but that Geoff refuses to get rid of even though no one has ever shown any interest in ordering one.

The Red Lion is where we first met Barry. Last man standing on pretty much our first shift, left alone in the booth furthest from the door and cradling the dregs of his pint as a busy Friday night ended. His eyes were glazed. He was wearing a tatty suit and a grimace as though waiting, just hoping for someone to say the wrong thing so that he could push what was left of his drink into their face, glass and all. I'd lost the coin toss but bottled it as I walked out from behind the bar, and so instead of reminding him we were closing I asked Barry if he would like a beer, on the house whilst me and John tidied up. This was an act of self-preservation (I'd have happily tossed him the keys to the pub door on my way out if he'd have asked), but from that moment on I was Barry's best friend. On the way home me and John had decided that this was a good thing, something to be nurtured so that should we ever need it, we'd have the muscle to back up our often too smart mouths. As time passed, though, and as Barry spent more time perched at the bar on the sixth stool, he did become sort of a friend. Not the 'let's give Bazza a call and see if he fancies a beer' type of mate but more the 'wonder if Barry's coming in tonight' kind. Eventually, inevitably, Barry felt enough kinship to confide and slowly he lowered his hard-man garb. He started telling us things, stuff like how much he hates his job and the scumbags he generally has to deal with. How he hates his mum too because she kept him off school to fold the clothes that she ironed when she was setting up her first business. How he blamed her for his dad leaving and how he wishes he'd listened at school so that he could've 'gone to uni like you two gay boys'. So yes, Barbara, I know your threat and I also know your little boy Barry very well, and this brings me to the most relevant and useful of the secrets that we share: Barry the Bailiff is crap at fighting and on the two occasions that debtors have called his bluff he's retreated after only a short flurry of fists, lips split or nose bloodied, and with none of the money owed having been collected.

That said, it isn't yet time to reveal my hand so still best to pretend for now, feign some level of fear at least whilst trying once more to negotiate a way through this.

'Aw, now come on, Barbara, there's no need for that. Look, once Geoff gets the sanitiser and hand cream bought, which he promised he would, then I'll be back at work and happy to discuss a payment plan to sort this out, but really, until then it's—'

'Bollocks to Geoff and bollocks to your lame-arse excuse. Believe me, your hands are going to get a whole lot sorer when you-know-who pays a visit. Let's just say that my associate can get very creative when it comes to persuading people to cough up.'

I'm not sure why she's avoiding telling me directly who will do what. I mean, it's not as if I'm recording this conversation, but there again, Barbara's no mug and maybe that's a lesson she's already learned the hard way. Actually, when I think about it, perhaps I will record her threats next time. Veiled or not, I reckon that it could be useful should I ever need a bit of leverage. To be fair to Barbara, though, I can see how frustrating this must be for a landlord, but her insistence that my reasons for not paying are nothing other than 'lame-arse excuses' makes it hard for me to sympathise and meet her halfway. After all, I'm just as much a victim here. I haven't packed in work just because I can't be bothered. All I'm doing is trying to follow two pieces of very simple advice.

Keep your distance and wash your hands, we're told.

No problem with the first bit. Geoff had soon realised that I was taking this virus seriously and after only half an hour of me refusing to serve people until they backed away he was happy enough to run a strip of yellow duct tape on the floor, one pace from the bar. Pretty much everyone respected the sign telling them to stay behind the line too, but the problem came once they'd reached over and grabbed their drink. It was then time to pay and this is the reason that Barbara is screaming at me now: the money tossed into the dish that I'd placed on the counter. Filthy, disease-ridden fivers dug from deep cesspit pockets by sweaty hands and with some dirty bastards even licking their fingers to help separate notes! Disgusting, and even without Covid I'd have been loath to touch it, but add a highly transmissible virus into the mix, along with a government warning – well, I was washing my hands hundreds of times a shift. A combination of cheap soap and a damp tea towel soon leached the protective oils out of my skin and by the end of the first night dry patches had appeared. Three days later and with supermarket shelves similarly stripped of the things needed to keep hands supple, the cracks had deepened and soon the pain became unbearable. Game over.

That was over a week ago and now, with a student loan blown and a zero-hour contract living up to its name, it's fallen to Barbara to take one for the team. She closes the conversation with a classic 'you have been warned' and then cuts the call. As Barbara's caller ID fades (actually a mugshot of a young Arnie made up in his Conan the Barbararian role, as John has nicknamed her) I see a message from my flatmate:

> Look like im stuck here for a while

> Why

> You not seen the news

Grabbing my tea, I move into the lounge and switch channels. Boris is on the Beeb, looking dishevelled as normal but also uncharacteristically stern. Our prime minister seems to be wrapping up whatever it is that he had to say, but the summary panel on the right-hand side of the screen tells me all I need to know. Non-essential businesses and schools closed, stay where you are, work from home if you can, and no social gatherings.

'Finally looks like they're taking this seriously then.'

My words are whispered into an empty room, but even though they are heard by no one they don't feel wasted and instead sound incredibly important, more so than anything I can ever remember saying. They have a weird effect on me too; on the one hand giving me a warm sense of satisfaction that I was right to follow the initial advice (ignore the snide scoffs and slowly shaking heads), whilst at the same time chilling me with an unnerving and unshakable feeling that something dark and terrible had entered my life. Something that right now was lurking outside my door.

No one in, no one out, not for at least three weeks.

Lockdown's upon us and I officially no longer pay rent.

2

The next morning brings a cloudless sky and a barrage of messages across all platforms. Insta can wait; I'm not in the mood for messages from celebrities assuring me that 'we're all in this together'. So condescending too, trying to mug us off by snapping selfies in the smallest, most humble room they have as if we don't know they live in acres of luxury. Next is Facebook and that takes only as long as the kettle needs to boil for me to filter through the 'oh my god!' brigade, hitting an appropriate amount of likes as I do. There is one post among all this faux panic that does grab my interest, though, and I make a mental to note to have a word with my next-door neighbour Matt (about the apparent shindig he's organised for tomorrow) next time I see him on his balcony. He has a table and chair there, set on the other side of a horizontal row of slick stainless-steel bars installed to keep balconies private. I have a similar furniture arrangement, pushed up against his, and this makes it ideal for playing cards or simply having a chat and a beer. Don't ask me why we meet through the railings like this rather than calling round, but we do, always have done since we first exchanged a nod and an 'alright' three months ago. To do anything different now would seem weird, like we had decided to take our relationship to another level. Must admit, though, it does feel like some kind of break up or betrayal as I drag my table away from the partition and position it in the opposite corner of my balcony, but that's what I do, putting at least four metres between me and him should he appear. Once settled I sip my coffee and take a look at my messages.

The first is from Barbara.

> Mr Liam Slater, please be advised that the recent decision by the UK government to enter a period of lockdown changes nothing. You remain in debt to MyPad rental agency in the sum of two months rent. This can be reduced by the retention of your deposit subject to a satisfactory inspection once your rental agreement terminates. Rgds

Delete.

The second is from John.

> Locking down with Sally might see you at matts tommo you can have my food but dont touch my stash

I feel bad for laughing, but seriously? He could have easily made it back from Salford last night but instead he decides to lock himself in a tiny flat twenty floors above a housing estate that's on the news more than Syria. She's dirty too, and not in a good way. Sally has a strange smell, but whenever I've nudged him, pointed and turned my nose up when she is distracted, he looks away and refuses to acknowledge the stinky elephant in the room. During their first week together I must have raised this at least four or five times when we were alone, but his defensive denials became so heated that they seriously threatened our friendship, so I stopped. For anyone, living with a person who has such a lack of personal hygiene would be a challenge, but for two-showers-a-day John? Yes, Sally is fit, but no way fit enough to keep him from eventually saying something, and once that's done he'll regret locking himself away with her, big time.

> Do I need to buy a wedding hat

>> piss off and be careful you dont sprain your wrist loser

It's a good point well made, and John's jibe puts a whole new slant on the mad dash for bog roll that's been the lead story all morning. It is also a huge reality check because not only does it go some way to explaining John's spur-of-the-moment decision to move in with Sally, more significantly it drives home to me the fact that this is really happening, that I am locked away on my own. Not for long, though, as it turns out; Matt's patio door announces his arrival with a metal-on-metal grinding screech that grabs my ears and turns my head.

'Morning, Liam, how's things in… what you doing all the way over there?'

Really, Matt?

'Social distancing, Matt. It's called social distancing. Which, to be honest, mate, is what you should be doing instead of organising a piss-up for tonight. So, thanks for the invite, but I'm out.'

Matt's lips tighten and he nods slowly. Recognition, perhaps, that I'm right and acceptance that he needs to reconsider his rash call for a lockdown party? Wildly optimistic this, as his pensive pause is taken only to allow the clumsy construction of what is the first of no doubt a thousand Covid jokes yet to come.

'You want social distancing? You should have said, pal! My sister's got a tape measure if you want two metre.'

'Very funny, but seriously, Matt, you can't have a party.'

'It'll be fine, Liam, don't sweat it, fella. It's not like I'm inviting my mum and dad. It's all young people, so no worries. You okay to grab some mixers?'

This is like talking to Barbara. Matt isn't listening and I really can't muster the energy this early, so I lie and tell him no problem.

'Well, if nothing else, I suppose it'll keep you busy today, getting ready for your bash.'

'Oh no, mate, I'm off to work in five. I'll ask Pete for an early finish, though. Means I'll have to invite the boring bastard, but hey ho.'

Matt's attitude is pissing me off. I'm pretty sure that he's seen the same news that I have, but for some reason he has decided that none of it applies to him. I should give him the benefit of the doubt, though, and so, as unlikely as it is that the message has passed him by, I check that my assumption is valid.

'You have seen the news, right? The bit about working from home if you can and non-essential businesses closing? Last I remember, you work in a place that makes tents, Matt, bleedin' tents, so I'm sorry to be the one who has to tell you, mate, but what you do ain't worth a shit!'

'Thanks, Liam, oh mighty and worthwhile one, love you too, but what you seem to be forgetting is that my company is literally called Outdoor Essentials. It actually has the word essential in it!'

'Essential if you're going camping! And look, I know that the advice has been a bit confused until now, what with the in then out and now in again, but unless Boris's next instruction is for everyone to shake it all about, then I'm pretty sure he isn't trying to set a world record for the most people doing the hokey pokey!'

'Well, whatever, but it's a tricky one. Some say it's best to stay in and others it's okay to go out and I need money, so for now…'

With this nonsense made-up fact and a shrug of his shoulders, Matt wins the argument. A smile and a thumbs-up denies me any retort. He drags the patio closed, gives a final shout to remind me about the mixers then off he goes to get ready for a world that he's convinced is the same as yesterday.

The world isn't the same. Everybody knows it, so why is Matt refusing to do what, at the end of the day, is a pretty reasonable request to stay at home? There has to be something more driving his disobedience than just raging against the machine. Does he not believe what we're being told about what's happening? Maybe that's a part of it because I must admit, when you break this down, strip it back to the very beginning it is an incredible thing to think that this all began with a mouthful of food. Imagine that, popping into KFC to grab a bite on the way home, chewing off a chunk of greasy, spicy meat and in that simple, everyday act setting in motion a series of events that would kill thousands, close borders, smash families apart and grind economies into the ground. I mean, if one bite of a burger or a chicken thigh or a bat wing can do all this then what else is possible? So, maybe that's it. Not disobedience but denial because in truth, once you admit that this is happening then you've no choice but to accept how ridiculously fragile our lives are.

This thought zones me out for a few moments and when I refocus I'm looking out on a vista that I rarely appreciate. Me and John paid a tad extra to have a corner flat and our balcony wraps around it. However, due to a sunny aspect and our relationship with Matt, any time we spend on the balcony is passed sat immediately outside the patio doors looking across at our apartment block's twin building which rises no more than fifteen metres away across a single row of parking spaces. Having shifted along to the outside corner for a change and being up on the third floor, I now get a great view of Woodlands Park. The council could never claim this to be the best kept green space in town, but I would argue that it is one of the most frequented. I often joined the throng of workers and students that cross it daily to board one of a procession of buses that wait there on the far side. During weekends the commuters are joined by rampant kids and strolling retirees, their fondness for the place evidenced by the large areas of grass that have been ploughed back to mud by knobbly tires, football boots and stout shoes. There are paths too, of course, but these are for the most part dangerous to use: cracked and gouged by neglect and barely connecting the roundabouts, swings and benches scattered around.

It's Wednesday. I check the time. Almost ten o'clock and the park should be empty, so I check again. Nine fifty-two, so why the hell is the park so busy! Mobbed by more people than you would normally expect to see on a bank holiday weekend; I start to count, but my rising anger stops me at seventy-five and that's all within fifty metres of the park entrance! There must be hundreds: strolling, chatting, sitting and just generally gathering, a herd of idiotic sheep grazing away happily, oblivious to the wolf that walks among them. Not only youths (which I kind of understand given their misconceived invincibility) but families too: mums and dads, grandparents kicking balls for kids or dogs to chase. As well as the view it offers, another advantage of the third floor is that it isn't so high that I can't shout down fairly easily and be heard. Focusing on the park entrance initially, I pick my first victims to chastise: a group of people who are stood around a bench with their backs turned.

'Hey, you lot! Yes, you, with the blue hoody. You and your mates need to go home, stay inside.'

I know they've heard me because pretty much all six of them have turned to see where the voice is coming from.

Not one of them, however, shows any signs of moving on, so I shout down again and ask them once more to follow the advice that we've all been given.

'Yeah, but like you say, it's just advice, innit, so you can do what you want with it, pal, but we're staying here.'

The man in the blue hoody is right, of course, and the mixture of defiant and disbelieving stares that I'm getting back from his mates makes me wonder if perhaps I am overreacting. After all, as strongly as it's been stressed in fine words and catchy straplines, stay at home unless you absolutely have to go outside remains advisory only.

'Okay, I get you, but really, mate, have a think about it, eh? Just because we don't live in China where they'd make you do it, staying inside isn't that hard, is it? I mean, this shit could get very real very quickly, so maybe it's good advice to take for now, yeah?'

Softening my tone and supporting his right to be confused seems to do the trick. There is some pointing as the group discuss where to go next, and then, as one, this loyal brotherhood nod their hooded heads and shuffle away, hands plunged in pockets, off to test their unshakable belief that youth and vodka will protect them. Only one remains, sat hunched forward on the bench.

'You should go too, pal.'

The man looks up, stares at me long enough to make me uneasy then, leaving a long pause between words, asks, 'Go where?'

'With your mates. Or if not then go home.'

'They're not my mates.'

His deliberately awkward attitude raises my voice back

up to somewhere just below a shout. 'Well, go ho…'

That's when I see it: the piece of cardboard lying on the ground by his feet. If there is writing on it I can't read what it says, but the message is loud and clear, and I feel awful. I change my tone for a third time, this time to something that I hope sounds apologetic and offer the best help I can.

'Look, there's a shelter on Whitworth Street. I'm sure they'll have done something for people in your situation, extra beds and stuff. Why don't you try there? I can ring them for you if you'd like.'

The man pushes on his knees and slowly stands. He takes a single but very purposeful step forward then lifts his head, locks his stare. I don't like this gesture. There is nothing particularly threatening about him (he has a kind face, open posture), but still, the stance he has taken feels like an act of defiance, as if he's trying to show me that he is my equal, which of course he is, and I'm confused by it. I mean, it's not as though I'm responsible for his misfortune. I'm not the one treading him down. Quite the opposite, in fact: I'm trying to help him yet still he stares, and whilst I am certain of my innocence here, a sense of guilt keeps me on the balcony looking down, holding his gaze for an uncomfortably long silence so that I can be sure he understands that I've seen him, that I know he exists whilst trying hard not to seem as though I am pitying him.

Finally he blinks and very calmly gives me his well-considered answer. 'Tell you what, how about you do give them a ring but ask them if you can go and stay there and then I can move into your place for a bit? How does that grab you, arsehole?'

The man's face and stance remain, but everything else about him changes. He isn't kind; he is calculating. He isn't helpless; he is very capable. He isn't benign; he is creepy and threatening. I no longer feel obliged to stand and be seen, so I turn away, an act that angers him instantly, and it isn't until I've closed the patio door behind me that he stops slinging insults up to my balcony. It takes a few more minutes for me to stop replaying them in my mind (some of the things he said were just outright threats) and it takes even longer for me to shake the feeling that it was a mistake to engage with him at all.

3

Up until I was five, Staff Sergeant William Peter Slater had been my father. I don't remember too much about the time that we spent together, barracked in Germany, but from what I've been told since (by family and friends and at least three of the hundred or so soldiers that he commanded) he was a top bloke with a sense of humour matched only by his sense of duty and loyalty.

My dad and mum had been abroad for almost twenty years when I arrived, only a couple of days after the millennium had ticked over. At forty years of age they were at that time considered quite old to be having their first kid. The army had been good to them, though, assigning larger accommodation in a quieter part of the base, but as Mum tells it, after three or four years it became clear that their situation wasn't sustainable. Unsurprisingly there had been the expected pressures brought to bear on a soldier's young family, not least Dad's deployment to Iraq. More insidious, though, had been the slow erosion of my father's career path. Before I was born that had been clear and firm, well signposted, but as I had grown so had the number of platoon or social events missed. The path had been eroded, worn away by the stamping, ambitious boots of younger men, and the signposts had become less easy to follow, obscured by huge question marks daubed across them by his commanders. The last time that I saw Staff Sergeant William Peter Slater was the day we left Germany to go back to Manchester.

I remember the first time I met the man that replaced him. I had been six years old, sat on the wall outside our terrace house waiting for his return. It had been Billy Slater's first day at the warehouse and as he stepped from the bus and crossed the road I smiled and waved. He didn't wave back; he just walked past me and entered the house. I've never forgotten how that made me feel, how I had been left in no doubt that I was to blame for the wreckage of his army career. We're good now, of course, have been for years, and even though we have never spoken of it I'm pretty sure that he remembers that day, that look as well as I do. The funny thing is that I've found myself thinking about that day quite a bit recently and I was working up to asking him directly about my part in him leaving the army, but that ain't happening now, at least not for a while. Dad's an emotional enigma at the best of times, like trying to read Braille wearing boxing gloves, so gauging his true feelings on Zoom is a nonstarter.

The screen blinks and Mum's face appears. She is sat awkward and stiff on the couch.

'Hi, Mum, you okay? Can you hear me alright? Where's Dad?'

'Hi, Liam, love, how are you? Yes, we're fine. Dad's here, right next to me but says he doesn't want to be on camera.'

Point proven, and I completely support his disdain for video calls. They are a complete pain in the arse, but for some reason, although nothing is really any different yet (it being only twelve hours since the world locked down), people now see video chat as the only way to communicate. Yesterday a phone call or a text was fine; today we have to watch jittering images of each other, smile and ask mundane questions to avoid brutally honest dead airtime. Here comes one now from my dad, as he feels obliged to butt in, unseen and with an agitation in his voice that tells me he's already sick of the pleasantries.

'Have you got plenty of food in, Liam? They say this could last a while and the less you have to go out the better.'

I haven't checked the cupboards yet, but I say yes anyway, which turns out to be the wrong answer. Rather than shut the question down I've managed to launch Dad into an endless inventory of Tesco's shelves; things that I must have and things I shouldn't. The most bizarre item on the don't list are bananas because 'they'll make other fruit go bad' and I can't be trusted to keep them separate apparently. Through all this he refuses to pause or come into camera, and so I nod and look at my motionless mum staring back at me. Eventually she's had enough too, but instead of interrupting him she decides to synchronise her mouth with his words. She nails it too and the effect is hilarious. It's only when she gets over-ambitious, begins to scowl and rock her head to his rhythm, that she is sussed.

'Well, you can mock me all you want, Brenda, but this is important.'

Time for me to wrap this up and I would have felt guilty for bailing out so abruptly but for the three sharp raps on the door that demand my attention. Mum protests, no doubt looking for a bit of moral support, but more knocks interrupt her plea and force me to garble a promise that I'll call tomorrow. I close the laptop and disconnect.

The chair I sit on is close to the door and in my haste to see who's behind it I have reached out and twisted the handle almost to the point of opening, realising my mistake only when the latch disengages. Quickly I release, push the door firmly so that it clicks back closed and then stand to ask who is there.

'It's me, you knobhead. You letting me in or what? We need to get ready to go to Matt's?'

'I've told you, John, I'm not going. And you shouldn't be either.'

John is cursing me, beneath his breath and barely audible so I can't hear exactly what he is saying. This is frustrating but at the same time a stroke of luck because the quiet enables me to hear the tell-tale jingle of keys being taken from a pocket. I draw the deadbolt.

'You're not coming in here either, especially having spent the night at Smelly's.'

'What did you call me!'

This voice isn't John's and although I don't see her being a part of his life for longer than lockdown lasts, I do feel bad about Sally hearing this. With nothing to lose, it's worth a shot at trying to recover, so here goes.

LOUTH LIBRARY SERVICE 217472

'Oh, hi, Smiley, I didn't know you were here. How's things?'

'Smiley? I heard you say smelly.'

'Oh no, god no, it was smiley. I called you smiley. That's what John always calls you and I guess it's stuck in my head. He loves your smile, always going on about it.'

He doesn't and he isn't. How could anyone love a smile so thin, so protective of teeth that you could only really be proud of on Halloween or at Troll Con? My deflection is successful, though, and earns John a big soppy aaaaaww from Sally along with an insistence that this is what he must call her from now on.

'Well, I think you're being a bit of a tar, but at least let me in to pick some gear up then. Two minutes tops.'

'No, John, you are not coming in, not for a second. I'd have to spend the rest of the night sanitising everything you touch, so no. Just tell me what you want and I'll put it on Matt's balcony.'

'Fine then! My dark blue jeans, that Diesel T-shirt you're always trying to nick and there's a rucksack full of washing next to my bed. Grab that and I'll wash it through at Sally's.'

'Er, 'scuse me, my name's Smiley, if you don't mind. And I don't have a washing machine.'

What follows is one of the most bizarre conversations I have ever heard a couple have. It begins with a rather shocked John checking that he had heard correctly, that the girl he is spending at least the next three weeks with has no means to clean clothes. Confirmed and so John moves on to denial, confident that Sally does in fact have a washing machine and that it's the big silver appliance tucked under the worktop next to the fridge. Nope, because it turns out that this is in fact an ice machine. Apparently the girls had been faced with a difficult choice when they were kitting out their flat. With no room for both appliances it was either buy the washing machine from Currys or have their friend (who runs the student union bar) drop off the ice machine that he was replacing. Their logic, flawed on an epic scale, had been this: why spend money on something you need when you can get something you don't need for free, especially if they both fit in the same gap? Finally a worried acceptance and an exasperated plan B from John.

'You better stick that big tin of Febreze in too, will you, Liam? Okay, Sally, let's go and party.'

I don't hear movement, a silence only explained when John invites his date a second time and Sally playfully puts her foot down.

'No, not until you call me Smiley!'

It's a cruel irony that Sally's southern accent and soft, lazy vowels makes it impossible for her to be properly understood, and so John's girlfriend is about to meet a whole room of new people with a broad, confident green grin through which she will introduce herself as Smelly.

I'm still laughing at this image on my way to John's room to get the things he needs. As I pass the kitchen I reach in, grab an apple from the fruit bowl and take a huge bite. The mush that fills my mouth is disgusting: a rotten, bitter and wholly unpleasant explosion of slime prepared by the evil banana lying beside it. Bending over the sink to empty and rinse my mouth I'm reminded once again that karma is not something that I should be messing with.

4

It's late when I eventually get around to packing some things for John. I've spent the evening on the settee in front of the TV trying to reconcile my decision to sacrifice the fun next door (so intense that it's vibrating crockery in the kitchen cupboards) for the greater good of doing bugger all. It's a genuine conflict, but I know I am right; every pundit on every news programme tells me so. Still, when I finally do drag my sulky arse from the living room, as I'm stuffing things angrily into party boy's rucksack, I find myself wondering if perhaps I should relent, maybe take John's clothes next door to give them to him personally? Of course I'll have to stay a little while if I do, it'd be rude not too, and perhaps, once there, my nagging social conscience will be drowned out by booming drum and bass, and, more than likely, my stiff resolve will be diluted to nothing more than an aftertaste by an even stiffer G&T. Right there, that would be the moment when I could claim my high ground, look down from my high horse and proclaim to everyone how well I'd done to stay at home for a day more than they did. The party will cheer, chant my name and then catch me as I leap to crowd surf from the dining table, carried aloft around the room like the hero I am!

So enticing is this image that I fully intend to draw back the deadbolt and end my lockdown and maybe I would have had it not been for glimpsing that hypnotic, spiky red ball turning slowly on my TV screen, sending cold shivers through me on my way to open the door.

'Stick to the plan, Liam, stick to the plan.'

As if rewarding me for being a good citizen, the universe tosses me a bone: the tell-tale grate and grind of a patio door opening means that some smoker or pot-head is stepping out onto the balcony next door. This will save me the embarrassment of having to wave and shout to try and catch the eye of one of the party people. I step outside, my night vision taking a moment to kick in, but as irises dilate so a figure is solidified from the gloom, standing in the shadows at the far end of Matt's balcony lighting a cigarette.

'Here, mate, can you do me a favour?'

The instant that the girl steps towards me, emerges from out of the dark corner, my voice softens and deepens. She is blonde and slim and a couple of inches shorter than me. As best as I can tell in the low light spilling from the party inside, she has a striking resemblance to Penny – the hot penny, though, and not the one from an episode of *Big Bang Theory* that makes you think hard about whether or not it's Penny or Bernadette who should get the top slot.

'Hi. Listen, bit cheeky, I know, but I wonder if you'd do me a solid? See, there's a friend of mine at the party and I have a bag of clothes for him. Any chance I can pass them to you?'

'Sure.'

The girl steps to the front of the balcony and reaches around the bars. I put the rucksack strap in her hand, check that she has a good grip and let go so that she can take it. She puts it down on the floor and as she steps back asks me why I'm not at the party. Tricky, this. I don't want her to think I'm some sad loser who hasn't been invited and I'm just as keen that she doesn't see me as some kind of goody-two-shoes coward, scared of a catching what for someone my age is likely to be nothing more than a sniffle and a cough. Being ill is the way to go, though, so I'll tell her it's my stomach, that I've eaten something a bit iffy.

'Oh, I was invited, but I'm feeling a bit—'

'Shit! You don't have symptoms, do you?'

Her panic is instant and genuine, and it reels her back into her corner. Surprising, this, for someone who has just stepped out of a packed room of sweaty revellers, and it takes me some very creative apple-based reassurance to coax her towards me again. This time the girl stops two paces short of the bars but importantly doesn't choose to go back inside. Instead, she drops her cigarette to the floor, stomps it out slowly with a twisting, lingering foot whilst telling me that her name is Jenny and that she works with Matt. Cigarette dealt with she looks up, flicks her hair from her face and asks me how long I've known him. This is good. With nothing to smoke, an interest in me *must* be Jenny's reason for staying here on the balcony and away from the party! I answer quickly, before she loses it.

'Three months or thereabouts, pretty much since he moved in, I guess. And you, Jenny, how do you know him?'

'Work. I run the reception at Outdoor Essentials. We sell all kinds of camping gear but mainly tents and stuff. No idea why, but our boss is in the party too so it feels more like a work do than a lockdown party. Not really enjoying it, to be honest. All Matt's got is neat vodka and gin, and I can't drink either on their own, but the bloke who was bringing the mixers is a no-show, selfish git so... Oh, bugger, that's you, isn't it? You're Lidl, the "neighbour who's terrified of catching a cold".'

There's no doubt that my cover is blown and my lie exposed, but did I hear her correctly?

'Lidl, did you say? Like the supermarket?'

'Yes, Lidl. Oh, by the way, that's your new nickname apparently. Short for lame dick Liam. So does it suit you, Lidl?'

The innuendo makes me blush, but it's weirdly welcome. I'm glad that she doesn't seem to be put off by what is turning out to be one hell of a Tinder profile:

Liam, twenty, an accomplished, small-dicked liar, a killjoy coward too and if that isn't enough to make you swipe right then don't forget that I can't be trusted and I'm only too happy to break a promise to a friend. Let's meet!

By the time I've finished beating myself up Jenny has moved the conversation on and thankfully isn't doubling down on her cheeky tease.

'You know, I don't think I'd have enjoyed myself even if I had managed to get drunk. I wasn't sure about coming, what with all the news and everything, but Matt convinced me, said that if the boss says we have to go to work and be near people then we might as well be with people and have fun after too, right?'

'Makes perfect sense to me, Jenny!'

Of course it doesn't. It's a ridiculous construct and I haven't changed my mind about this in the last few hours, but hey, I'm a lying bastard now, so why not use my new-found superpower for good? I am intrigued by what she said about her boss, though, that he had insisted they should go to work because I'd been angry at Matt when I believed that it was a choice he had made. Maybe I'd been a bit hasty and unfair if he was simply doing what his boss had told him to.

'So your boss said you have to go to work, did he?'

'Yes. He reckons that we're considered essential. Our company has literally got the word essential in it, he said. Did I tell you we make tents?'

Times like this can bring out the worst in the exponents of capitalism, chasing profit at any cost, but as much as I despise Jenny's boss, with my next words I join him on the dark side.

'Well, when this is all over Jenny, we are going to need tents, that's a fact. Be a lot of people heading for the hills after being cooped up for so long.'

She finishes her cigarette and picks up the rucksack. 'I guess so. Well, it's back to the party for me. Nice to meet you, Lidl.'

With that Jenny is gone. My attraction to her keeps me on the balcony a few minutes more, but there is no romcom paper plane with her number scribbled on it flung my way, so I turn to leave. That's when I notice the old man standing on his third-floor balcony opposite.

'You doing okay there, fella?'

The old man remains silent, nods once and then he too abandons me back to my lockdown.

5

One of the first things that me and John bought when we moved into the flat was a glossy whiteboard. We fixed it to the wall opposite our bedrooms. The idea was that we would collaborate there to solve the various math problems set by our tutors and it worked really well.

Having a shower and noticed how div grad curls marshal the billowing steam to dump entropy on a chilled mirror? Grab a towel and a marker pen as you leave the bathroom and sketch out a vector field for the other to check out. Had that dream again about your mate's mum, the one where you've been a naughty boy and made to stay back to watch her reconstruct a classic proof of the irrationality of $2\sqrt{}$ on the blackboard whilst wearing lace lingerie? Well, scribble down what you can remember on your way to make toast (but under no circumstances sign it off with 'special thanks to Mrs Kelly! TOP MILF!').

Feeding off each other's inspiration like this has no doubt made a huge contribution to the academic success that both me and John have had, but in the one and a half years since that board was first screwed to the wall, I can't recall it ever being used to crack a problem as complex as the one which faces me now. For at least half an hour already this morning I've stared at the question scrawled in capitals across the top of the board and I am no closer to solving it. I know that there must be a solution, but what the hell am I missing! Stepping back I read the question again, out loud, along with the two possibilities that I initially wrote down when I first defined the problem.

THINGS TO ASK MUM AND DAD
1 What Time You Having Dinner
2 How Is Granddad

And that's it! That's all I have! It feels more like a track list for Elton John's next Christmas album rather than topics to discuss with loved ones. I'll leave it there for now in the hope that its persistent mocking during the day will be sufficient to break my mental block before the evening call.

I've already spent too much time just staring at it, so much, in fact, that I'm not the first to sit with a coffee on the balcony. Matt is already there, large orange juice and a bacon sandwich to soothe his hangover.

'Good night, was it?'

'Oh man, it was a belter, so funny. You missed a good night, Liam.'

'Don't you mean Lidl?'

Matt almost chokes on his butty. 'Hey, listen, that wasn't me, mate, no way. It was your flatmate.'

'Figures.'

'And whilst we're on the subject, does he have Covid or what? I mean, that girl he was with, a bit ripe, isn't she?'

Matt is kind of joking, but maybe having the virus wipe out his sense of smell could explain John's inability to recognise Sally's whiff. Timing checks out. Who's to say he hasn't been walking around full of Covid for weeks already! He could have been, totally asymptomatic too which means that I won't know if I'm infected or not for at least another ten days or so! I think about this whilst I sip coffee. In my periphery I notice the homeless guy who I'd had a run in with yesterday sat on his bench. I regret the glance I throw his way; he is staring at me with such cold eyes, obviously holding on tightly to the despise that he inexplicably developed for me during our last encounter.

Turning away, twisting so as to more fully face and engage Matt, I feel anxiety churning my stomach, and whilst this may be in some part due to the man's hateful glare I have to be honest and admit to myself that I'm actually nervous about the answer to the question I'm about ask.

'That Jenny girl, your receptionist, she seeing anyone?'

'No, mate. Why? You interested?'

'She seems nice, yeah. We only talked for a little while, but yeah, she seems nice.'

'Go for it, pal. You want me to put a word in?'

'No, oh god, no! No. I'll follow up when I see her next.'

Matt takes a bite of his sandwich, chews, swallows and then rips another bigger mouthful from it. He's on his way to a third, but I don't have the patience and I need him back on topic.

'So what you reckon?'

Matt's head is lowered over his plate, mouth open and poised, ready to attack the bread gripped in his hands, egg and brown sauce dribbling through his fingers. He flicks his eyes my way, annoyed by my intrusion and seemingly having already forgotten about my romantic intentions to the girl, so I have to remind him.

'About seeing Jenny, I mean. When do you think that might be?'

'How the hell should I know? When this shit is all over, I guess, or… hang on a minute, Lidl, you want me to have another get-together, don't you? Well, you've changed your bleedin' tune, Mr "you're all going to die". But panic not, my horny little hypocrite, we were thinking about making it a weekly affair, so keep next Wednesday open.'

Pointless to deny that manipulating Matt into organising a repeat party was my plan, but he is wrong to think that I'm going to reset my quarantine clock to attend it, just so I can take a shot at someone I've only chatted with for five minutes. Thinking about it, a second rendezvous on the balcony is probably a better bet anyway. It's already kind of our thing, our place. And the bars dividing us add a dash of danger, as though our meeting there is somehow taboo. More importantly, my refusal to go to the party (which, if I did go, would in truth come off as very needy) will go some way to repairing what must be my woeful character in her eyes. Yes, this time Jenny would think of me as a man of principle: steadfast in my commitment to the common good, righteous in my denial of the pleasure promised by this forbidden fruit.

'Makes no difference to me, Matt, I still won't be coming round.'

'Well, if you change your mind this one's going to be fancy dress, a Covid-themed party, so wear something… actually, what the hell is a Covid costume?'

He isn't asking me. Matt has finished his breakfast and is on his way back inside, no doubt to watch the news to try and get some ideas as to what to wear next week. Time for me to go back inside too. My chair scrapes as I push it back to stand and gather my breakfast pots. Three seconds following this noise there is a second one, a soft thud, and I immediately understand what has made it. I turn and an empty balcony wall confirms my fear. Grabbing the concrete with both hands I lean over it to see where the trainers that I had been drying there have landed.

'Shit.'

I was hoping that perhaps they would have bounced close to one of the bushes outside the landscaped entrance of my apartment block, but they haven't; both shoes are there, remarkably close together, lying in the middle of the pavement and in plain view. They won't survive long exposed like this, not around these parts, and I scan the road, desperate to see someone I know, someone who could toss them back up, but the street is deserted.

'Shit, shit!'

Panic. The homeless guy is moving, rising wearily from his seat and then striding purposefully out of the park and towards my shoes. He picks them up with his grubby hands, then inspects them as if he's in Footlocker and can't decide whether to get the Pumas or go back and try once more the Adidas ones that he liked earlier. I need to act, and quickly too, so, left with no choice, I put my trust in humanity and call down.

'Here, mate, do you think you could throw them back up to me?'

Funny guy, this. He's turning slowly and deliberately, looking around, pointing at himself in a very exaggerated manner as if to say 'are you talking to me?'.

'Okay, okay, I get it and look, I know we got off on the wrong foot yesterday, but fairs fair, eh? Please, mate, I'm asking nicely. Please just throw my trainers back.'

He stops spinning and points directly at me with one hand, holds my trainers aloft with the other. 'Your trainers, did you say? Oh no, my privileged friend, you are mistaken. These are my trainers. I have a receipt and everything. Why don't you come down and I'll show it to you?'

He really is a grade A arsehole, this bloke.

'Look, I can prove they're mine if I have to. They've got my initials marked on the insole.'

'You're gonna get the coppers then? Go on, give 'em a ring. I don't think they're too busy at the moment. It's just a good job I wrote my initials in my trainers too for just such an occasion, so let's see.'

Whilst he calls my bluff he looks inside one of the shoes. 'Yep, these are mine. LS, Larry Smith. That's me.'

My heart sinks. I know this is game over, his piss-taking grin forcing me to accept that I have no choice but to say goodbye to my favourite footwear. I should go back inside now, deny the twat any more pleasure, but I can't let this go without telling him what I think.

'You are, quite simply, a lying knobhead, pal, and you deserve what you get.'

Larry Smith is triggered by something in this, explodes

into a vile and violent rant. 'Yeah! And who's gonna do that then? You? You gonna come down and sort me out, Mr Liam Slater of apartment three, fourteen Paradise Heights? Yeah, that's right, pal, I know who you are, so come on then, come on down and let's see what you've got!'

How the hell does he know my name?! And why is he calling me out, daring me to follow through on a threat I didn't even make? I didn't threaten him! Did I? For Christ's sake, I was talking about his predicament, which admittedly was a very low blow, but still, surely he understood that? No way was I implying that there'd be consequences, that I would resort to violence! I'm not Barbararian, for god's sake, sending my brutish son round to recover her debts! Jesus, I mean, as brazen as this lowlife's thievery is and as angry as it makes me, I would never ever resort to brawling to solve our differences.

Although, let's not be too hasty here.

After all, he started this. He is the one making all the threats and he is the one who has nicked my Pumas. Barry does owe me a favour too, if not for a direct quid pro quo then at least some demonstration that he values our friendship. No harm in asking and so, once back inside, I grab my phone from the low table in front of the settee.

How you doing.
Business slow I guess.
Listen I have a favour to ask but rather not text it.
Can you come over when you have a mo buzz me
and ill explain over the intercom

The intercom, that's how Larry Smith knows my name! It's right there, typed onto a sticky label next to the apartment number outside the main door. Good, that's a hell of a relief, I must say. It's one thing to feel menace, but when the someone doing it knows your name, calls it out, then the level of disquiet jumps as if increasing their voodoo hold over you just as a lock of hair or a drop of blood might. Well, you don't know me, do you, Larry Smith? All you know is how to read and count floors and doors, and this time tomorrow I will have my shoes back.

6

I'm thankful that it's Matt's day off and that he's having a lie-in. I don't much feel like a breezy chat this morning, glad of the time alone with my coffee and thoughts. Often when I get down like this it's hard for me to put my finger on the why, but today there is no doubting the reason: last night's Zoom session with Mum and Dad.

Rather than easing the family into a comfortable and bland schmooze, my dependably benign question about dinner time seemed to have festered during the last twenty-four hours, becoming rancid and rammed with controversy, because apparently Mum and Dad can't agree on what to eat or when to eat it. Dad, still refusing to sit in view of the camera, had taken huge offence when Mum announced that she had started defrosting a bolognaise without asking him. Try as we might, we couldn't console him and even Mum's 'whats-a-tomata-wit-a-you-a' pun didn't diffuse Dad's irrational huff. Okay, I didn't actually hear him get up and leave the settee, but he might as well have done because I didn't hear him speak again, not even to say goodbye.

It wasn't this lack of reconciliation with Dad that gave me a restless night, though; it was the conversation started by my second question which I interjected in an effort to change the subject. I wish I'd never brought it up, written it on the bloody whiteboard. When I asked how Granddad was Mum explained that physically he was doing great but that his memory seemed to be worsening with each visit. I had to agree; I had no choice but to lie about the last time that I'd called round to see him. I told her it had been the day before lockdown started and that I had noticed the same meandering mind. The truth is that the last time I had seen my granddad was over eighteen months ago.

It had been the day that me and John found the flat. On the way home from uni I had convinced him to take a detour so that I could drop off a ninetieth birthday card and a bag of Werther's Originals at Granddad's care home. I left John sat on the wall outside to enjoy his hard-negotiated booty: a cheeseburger and a promise that I'd only be five minutes, tops. Three minutes into the visit and I was already both annoyed and bored. Annoyed because whilst sucking too hard in my effort to create a perfect hole in the centre of one of those sickly sweets, I had snapped it in half. Bored because I had nothing in common with this old man sat on his white orthopaedic chair next to a dusty window. My sense of duty took a final, lethal blow when for the second time he asked me how I was doing at school and if I had a girlfriend. Standing to leave (it would take another minute of goodbye smiles to get to the door), that's when I noticed the huge advertising hoarding on the far side of the park, telling me that Paradise Heights was open for business. Two-

and three-bed modern apartments for rent, it said, ideally located for the city and the shops, and the artist impression promised me that once there I would be among respectable, professional people. I would chat to handsome, strong-jawed lawyers whilst standing next to tropical shrubs and I would wave at beautiful blonde doctors calling my name from their sleek bright white balconies.

I fell for it, bought the dream. Yes, I have on occasion stopped to talk with people at the shrubs, but it's been mainly heavily tattooed council workers, demanding that they clear the thorny weeds, and yes, I do have one of those balconies, but it's off-white render falls in clumps that have to be swept up every time it rains too hard. Oh, I am definitely living the dream! But this morning I have even more reason to regret the decision to rent here. In particular I rue that coin toss, the head not tail that convinced me and John to stump up an extra twenty quid a month for a corner unit. Not because of the extra wall area (and therefore sweeping duties) that this gets you, no. It's this new view from the balcony that I now wish I'd never seen.

Beyond the slender silver trunks of the beech tree grove that lines the right-hand side of Woodlands Park, I can see a heavily barred blue gate. It opens onto a short, narrow path that gives access to the green space for those inmates who are able and trusted enough to leave Granddad's care home and wander there. Despite its proximity I have never once taken the time to go and lean on that gate, to ask one of the carers if Norman Wallace is up and about, if he fancies a cuppa and a chat. The exact opposite, in fact. I've consciously avoided it, walked other paths so as not to be

40

spotted. That's why I feel so awful this morning; for the past eighteen months I have actively denied the fact that my granddad even exists.

God, I hate this virus! Not because it forbids me from doing something to fix this, from going and sitting with Granddad and scrubbing away my guilt but because if it wasn't for corona, if it wasn't for social distancing, I would never have moved my chair along the balcony and so I wouldn't be able to see that damning blue gate right now.

'You looking very pensive this morning, pal. Everything okay?'

So far down, I hadn't even heard the grate and grind of Matt's arrival. I force a smile, take a deep breath and answer him. 'I'm fine, mate. And you?'

'You can tell me if you want, Liam. Look, I know I wind you up a lot, but I can listen too, be serious when I need to be.'

This is an unexpected side of Matt, bringing me delight and trepidation in equal measure. It must have felt like this for those ten-year-olds getting invited to a sleepover at Neverland: you really want to see what's inside but you also know that once Mummy and Daddy leave then the popmeister's going to be naked moonwalking into your bedroom. Only one way to find out if I'm talking to Matt or Michael, I guess, so here goes.

'Okay. Well, I was just thinking about my granddad. He's in a home not far from here, but I was talking to Mum last night and it made me think what a selfish bastard I've been, not bothering to go and see him and all that. Been nearly two years.'

Matt comes to the bars, takes one in each hand and presses his face up against them as though he too is imprisoned by guilt. He doesn't speak until we lock eyes and I get the impression that he does indeed have something to say, something he thinks might help.

'Want my advice, Liam? Don't beat yourself up but also don't let yourself off the hook too easy either. Yes, you could say that grannies and granddads aren't our responsibility, and you'd be right. But what is our responsibility is to simply remember. Remember to let them know that we value them every now and again. Remember to make sure they know that we haven't forgotten them. And I'm saying this from personal experience, mate, trust me.'

'Why, what happened with you?'

'I did the same as you, mate. Grandma Jones was the last one standing, but even though she was alone and only lived two streets away, I was always too busy to call in. I always found an excuse, always had summat better to do, even if it was just doing nothing. I mean, how bad is that? How can doing nothing be more important than giving your granny a visit and a smile? I tell you, you have got to promise yourself to go visit him when this is done or you will regret it. You're lucky, though, because unlike me, it's not too late for you.'

'Shit, Matt, I'm sorry to hear that.'

Even as I offer my condolences I am pricked by my initial suspicion about Matt's ability to sympathise, niggled too by a feeling that I've heard this story before, its punchline delivered by a comic team captain on one of those supposedly improv'd satirical news shows.

'Hang on, is this the bit where you tell me that she isn't dead but that she's won the lottery?'

Matt steps back from the bars, wide-eyed, hands raised to head height as if he'd been shot. 'Wow! You certainly know how to make someone feel shit about trying to help you, Lidl. Okay, true, she isn't dead. Miserable old cow'll live longer than Dracula, mate, sat in her pink room with her bright-red lips. True too that she's cut me out of her will, but I ain't going to lose sleep over a twenty per cent share in a greasy short bread tin full of old pound notes. No, the point I'm trying to make is that it's too late for me because, quite simply, I genuinely don't care anymore. But the fact that you're sat here with a face like a vegan chewing bacon fat means that you are ashamed and that you do care. It means that it isn't too late for you and your granddad, Liam.'

Damn, this is actually good, solid, insightful advice! I really do feel better. Not about myself yet, I have behaved despicably, but the future does look brighter for me and Granddad. This is my pledge to both of us: as soon as this is over and it's safe for us to meet, I am going to stand at that blue gate and wait for him there.

'That's assuming, of course, that the old bugger survives this mess, 'cos if he dies before you get to him then you're gonna be guilt tripping for a long, long time, Lidl.'

And just like that, I'm back sucking bacon.

7

Yesterday didn't get any better and I was glad when it ended.

The call with Mum and Dad had been uncomfortable to say the least. They seemed to be in a better mood but I wasn't, so it was quite a stilted affair that didn't last more than a few minutes. I had hogged the conversation, spent most of it asking my mum questions about her dad until she finally asked why I was so interested. I felt my lies being exposed so I broke the connection.

Barry did eventually reply to my text but only to say that, whilst he's happy to help, he is busy and won't be free for a day or two. So that's another morning at least that I'll have to spend watching the tramp strut around in my best trainers. Each time he sees me looking in his general direction, Lying Larry Smith pretends not to notice me, but I am sure that he does because he always makes a point of raising a foot onto the bench to adjust the laces or simply just stroke my shoe. That's what he's doing now: spitting on a piece of tatty cloth and rubbing pretend dirt from the side of his left foot. I let my gaze linger, look away too late and as he raises his head we connect.

'You know what I really hate, Liam?'

Ignore him, he's not worth it.

'I hate it when people don't pick up their dog mess. Don't you? Hey, Liam, I'm talking to you! I said, don't you hate all that dog crap people leave lying about?'

Drink your coffee, Liam, don't even give him the satisfaction of a second glance. For a little while my turn-the-other-cheek tactic seems to work and he remains quiet, but my self-congratulation is premature and a minute or so later he starts prattling again. In his silence he has moved away from the bench, his voice now nearer, rising up from more or less directly in front of me.

'They just leave it lying around for any poor sod to stand in. Disgusting, don't you think?'

I double down on my phone, scroll through my WhatsApp messages again, but there is nothing there interesting enough to prevent my eyes from drifting beyond the screen and taking a peek at my nemesis, standing on the opposite side of the car park. He is balanced on one leg, crane like with one foot hovering over a brown splodge of what I can only assume is dog mess.

'Oh no, it looks like I'm going to step in some shit, Liam. All over my new trainers too!'

One hundred and ten quid those trainers were. Probably the most expensive thing I've ever bought and it's hard for me to stop myself from exploding as this lowlife twists and squidges that turd with first the left and then the right shoe. Those pristine hard court soles! Those finely engineered treads, specifically designed for a superior grip, now being packed with all that stinky crap. By the time Barry finally gets them back to me, all that minging dirt will have dried solid, impossible to ever get clean. God, I really do hate him!

From around the corner to my right there is sudden commotion. At first it's just gruff, loud noise, but as it gets nearer and clearer I can discern voices, crude and violent threats bawled at whoever the gang of thugs are chasing. Running scared, the victim is the first to come into view. A young lad, no more than sixteen, and he looks terrified, makes the mistake of trying to get away and at the same time check behind. Stumbling, arms flung forward, he hits the ground hard then rolls onto his back, prepares to defend himself from the fists and feet that no doubt are about to descend on him. I can see that he is Chinese, looks a bit like the kid who delivers my char siu pork on a Thursday night.

The others arrive.

'Hey! You lot! Just leave him alone! Just because he's Chinese, you racist scum! He's as English as you are and this corona shit has nothing to do with him, you bleedin' idiots!'

Three boys and a girl surround their prey. They continue to scream at him and ignore me. The tramp finishes mashing the turd and moves towards the crowd, but predictably he stops five strides away, with no intention of intervening.

'Right, you lot, I've called the police, so just leave him alone and do one!'

This gets their attention. As one they look up at me and

the girl speaks. 'Good. How long did they say they're going to be?'

'Hey, don't get cocky! They'll be here soon enough. What you're doing is unforgivable. It's people like you that give our country a bad name with your ignorant, racist intolerance. You should be ashamed!'

'I should be ashamed?! You need to get your facts straight, mister. For one, I'm not ignorant. I'm a final-year student at St Mary's and I'm sitting on an offer from King's College to read neuroscience. That's all about brains and stuff so if you ever find yours I'd be happy to take a look at it. Secondly, and you'll have to trust me on this, I come from a very very diverse gene pool, so if I was inclined to be racist I reckon I could choose to discriminate against pretty much any ethnicity. See the paradox, moron? Discrimination against everyone, equally? But more importantly, and here's the kicker, this poor defenceless lad on the floor that you're so concerned about is a bloody little thief who's just snatched my phone on the bus.'

Lying Larry Smith is grinning as he chooses this moment to step forward. He drapes an arm around the young black lad who is nearest to him then addresses the group, angrily pointing at me as he speaks.

'So when you think about it, who's the real bigot here? I mean, he's the one who for no reason tarred you lot as racists. He's the one who can't seem to see a Chinese person without thinking Covid carrier. Not only that, he's also quite happy to assume that this fine young man is a thug, just because he's a different ethnicity, I'll bet! What's next, Liam? Why not accuse him of spreading ebola too, eh?'

'Why the hell are you getting involved?!'

The tramp steps further forward to stand alone in front of the teens. This is the closest that he has ever been to me. There is evil mischief in his face; it is, quite frankly, chilling. I can see that he has a scar, starting in the corner of the left eye then disappearing into his beard. He sweeps an arm behind him, playing to the crowd and signalling for them to be quiet. A deep breath is drawn and then he speaks, each syllable articulated with confidence, not at all what you'd expect from someone who lives on a bench with a piece of cardboard at his feet.

'As Edmund Burke once said, the only thing necessary for the triumph of evil is for good men to do nothing. That, my fascist friend, is why I am getting involved.'

The girl claps slowly, encouraging her entourage to do the same. The applause builds further as someone on a balcony above starts to clap too! Even the Chinese kid is clapping now, pausing only to pat the tramp on his back, the two of them already as thick as thieves apparently. Swept up in the moment he reaches into his pocket, takes the stolen phone and gives it back to the girl. Lying Larry Smith grabs the kid's shoulders, spins him around into a hug and shakes him like some Baptist minister who's just exorcised a demon. He is so full of shit but still the applause amplifies as yet more balconies join in.

'Don't clap him! He's a scumbag, trust me on this!'

My plea is ignored and, if anything, has the opposite effect, spurring on a surge of louder claps and earning me a second, scolding monologue from the girl.

'My god, you are something else! Such a bigot! For your

information, misfortune doesn't make a person a scumbag, you arsehole. Hey, here's an idea. Why don't you try walking in his shoes for a day and see how you feel?'

'Oh, I would bloody love that! And believe me, pal, I will be walking in your shoes, and a lot sooner than you think, knobhead!'

I've lost it, I know I have, and as I scream at the tramp the girl shakes her head and beckons to her friends that their work here is done and it's time to leave. They do so, the pickpocket tagging along behind, seemingly forgiven, replaced by me as the villain of the piece. I am fuming at what just happened here, but then the Chinese lad stops, asks his new friends to wait for him. He jogs back, stands next to the shrubs and looks up.

'Hey, I just wanted to let you know…'

The lad pauses, more than likely embarrassed by what he has to say to me. I'm eager to save some face here though, get at least some recognition of my efforts to defend this little shit so rather than walk away I jump in, urge him to speak up and reassure him that we're cool.

'Yeah, whatever, dude. Like I said, I just wanted to let you know that we're still delivering, that's all. Look us up on Deliveroo. Oh, and don't forget to use discount code, SORRY4COVID.'

He turns then jogs on to catch the others up and whilst I should be mad, should be ranting after him, I can't help but smile. Unjustly cast as the villains of the piece by every world leader outside of Beijing, the boy's family could have easily buckled under the huge weight of savage public opinion, understandably cowered from the toilet-roll hoarding morons who scream profanities across the aisle at them. Yet they haven't. Instead they've decided to not only accept and even forgive people's fear but to use it; spice it up with humour and just enough tongue-in-cheek contrition to create a sweet-and-sour gesture that, I reckon, will go a long way to pulling our community back together.

8

Only once the car park and balconies have emptied can I bring myself to skulk back inside the apartment. My trainers are crammed with crap and my reputation is bruised, but on the plus side there is a complimentary portion of fried rice waiting for me online. That's the first thing to do: order dinner for tonight. The second thing is to print my email address and mobile number in huge bold letters, split across five pages of A4. These I tape to the inside of the patio door so that they can be clearly seen from across the way.

The idea of these poster-sized contact details is that the old bloke on the opposite balcony might read them and reach out. He had witnessed the debacle in the street, and when it was all done and dusted I had noticed two things that intrigued me enough to want to know more about him.

First thing had been his apparent inability to speak. After the car park had cleared I had called across the void, thanked my neighbour for not clapping along with the rest of them, but he hadn't replied. Instead he had simply motioned an open hand across his mouth and throat. I suspect that he was trying to communicate an inability to shout back to me, maybe he can't talk at all, who knows, but it had seemed a genuine attempt to connect, make me understand his predicament. Now, if he has a phone or a computer and feels so inclined, he can get in touch. I hope he does because above all else, it had been the second thing I'd seen that really grabbed my attention. It was a gun! A real-life shotgun! Sat in plain view on the balcony wall, it was, a double-barrelled defence, locked and loaded should the hoo-hah in the car park escalate his way. At least I'm ninety per cent certain that's that what it was, although admittedly he never raised it or butted it into his shoulder to sight anyone below. Still, even the possibility that someone the same age as Granddad has a lethal weapon and is, I assume, ready to use it in the event that he should need to hold his high ground… wow! Strange times had gotten a whole lot stranger in that moment and I'm so buzzed by this development that I know I won't be able to calm fully until I've found out what the score is. Lest I forget, I go to scribble a reminder on the whiteboard.

gun – old man?

Whilst at the board I'm reminded how abruptly my last chat with Mum had ended, and as I've got my laptop open, now seems a good a time as any to get my daily duty done. It's a bit earlier than usual and so it takes a little longer for them to accept the call, but Mum eventually does.

'Oh, hello, Liam, this is a nice surprise. You're calling early, aren't you? Everything okay?'

'Yes, it's all good, Mum. You okay? You too, Dad?'

'Oh, your dad's not here, love, he's out.'

'Out! What do you mean, out? Out where?'

'Don't panic, he's not out out, just not in the house. He's in his shed.'

Dad insists on calling his bolthole a shed. It isn't, by any stretch of the imagination. A shed is a ramshackle pile of re-purposed pallets, nailed and screwed together to form a large box with a porous door that doesn't quite close and a window frame recovered from the local tip. It's where men keep garden tools and a small beer fridge. The brick-built monstrosity that my dad created (the first big job undertaken when we moved back from Germany) stretches almost the full length of our back yard. To this day, every time I walk past road works or a building site, the smell of peaty clay reminds me of that summer when my dad's mates arrived carrying shovels and beer to dig deep slit trenches for the concrete foundations needed to support bricks and timbers, bury cables and pipes. Dad still insists it's a shed, though, makes a humourless point of correcting us whenever we tease him about his holiday home, and on the two occasions that we have had new neighbours move in, he has earnestly briefed us to be sure that we refer to it as 'a shed and only a shed'. I presume that this is to give us credible deniability, should we be overheard and the council planners come a-snooping, following up on a complaint.

As it always has done, the key to the shed door hangs on a hook in the kitchen, but I've only ever taken it a handful of times. I do remember seeing tools in there, presented neatly on hooks fixed to the wall behind a work bench. Other than that, to my mind the rest of the things don't belong in a shed at all. Don't get me wrong, putting bits of old furniture in sheds is common practice, but the stuff Dad used to kit out his den, despite being old and obviously junk, never felt 'cluttery' enough. Whilst the look falls well short of shabby chic, the ambience of the interior is closer to that of a room in a house and, to be more specific, a soundproofed room in serial killer's basement. It's a place where, yes, you would put plastic sheets down on the wooden floor, but not to catch drips of varnish as you renovate a table, more likely to prevent blood from seeping in to the planking whilst you're dismembering a prostitute. Instead of a battered radio there is a well-cared-for record player, ideal for playing those scratchy old 45s and dancing around your victim, menacingly explaining which bits you're going to slice off next. The turntable sits on top of one of those double drawer cabinets, made in the seventies from Formica laminate. It's chipped at the edges but still easy to wipe down. Either side of this, Dad has placed large, comfy lounge chairs, one blue and one orange, somewhere to crash and weep, perhaps, as you repent the blood on your hands. There was the obligatory fridge too, of course, but whenever I looked inside it had been chilling not beer but weirdly only foil-topped fizzy wine and, on one occasion, an open box of Terry's All Gold chocolates. At the far end of the room a tall, antique wardrobe is tucked tight in against the wall. It is padlocked but with no key that I could ever find, so I presume that the things inside it must be precious, power tools, probably. Finally, opposite the wardrobe stands the most striking and bizarre piece of furniture of the lot: a full-length mirror, pivoted in an elaborately gilded wooden frame. My mum always said that the mirror was being stored there, would be moved to their bedroom once they had decorated, but I never saw it in the house.

When my thoughts stop wandering around the shed and turn back to Mum she is busy defending her husband, bemoaning the fact that people need to remember that everyone needs a little alone time. Her tone is sharp, as if I had accused Dad of some selfish act. I hadn't, of that I'm sure, because one thing that I have learned during this first week of my lockdown is that the freedom to be alone, quiet and reflective, and without being mithered, without being constantly asked 'what you thinking?' or 'are you feeling okay?' is really important, yet somehow has become undervalued, even maligned in our society. Today we're told that we have to talk, we have to open up and tell people stuff that really is none of their business. If we don't, if we keep things inside, then we are either having a mental meltdown or being just plain rude. I'm pretty sure that's why Dad is in the shed now because to be brutally frank, as much as I love my mum I'm not sure that I could spend more than a few days chatting about the inane and being chastised every time I answer her with a grunt.

My phone is buzzing and I can see that it's Barry.

'Listen, Mum, sorry to cut you short but I have to take this call. Love you and say hi to Dad.'

I close the laptop and swipe my phone.

'Hey, Barry, how you doing?'

'We're doing okay, I suppose. Business is slow, though, and—'

'Great, that's great. Listen, are you available today?'

'Yeah, I can pop round now if you like. What is it that you need again?'

I explain. About the tramp that has stolen my trainers, the piss-taking, the veiled threats and how much I hate him. I probably go on a bit too much because when I'm done talking Barry is really riled up.

'And where can I find this arsehole again?'

'In the park. Go in through the entrance near my flat then turn immediately left. He'll be there, about twenty metres along the path, sat on a bench. Brown jacket, big beard. You can't miss him.'

'My left or yours?'

What? Did he just ask me which left or did I hear him wrong? Then the penny drops, the fact that Barry has only ever stood facing me across the bar and that maybe this is the reason for his confused, ridiculous question, but as tempted as I am, I don't have the time to belittle my halfwit henchman.

'Your left Barry, always your left. And listen, I want you to be aggressive, really frighten this bloke, yeah? And also, do you have a mask? Might be an idea to wear one just in case he gets in your face. Better safe than sorry.'

'I think so, I'll have a look. Just so we're clear, how far do you want me to go?'

'Like I say, I want him scared enough that he'll give you my shoes and also think twice about messing with me, but don't get physical. I don't want violence. When you've got them off him just toss them up onto my balcony as you go past. I'm going to be waiting inside. If he sees me he'll only act up. Okay?'

'No worries, Liam, consider it done.'

'Cheers, Barry, I owe you one, mate.'

I am very, very pleased with myself. In about an hour's time not only will I have my beautiful trainers back, but importantly too, some kind of order will be resumed. Lying Larry Smith will be put back in his box and my balcony life will return to normal. All that I have to do now is stretch out in front of the TV and wait for my plan to be executed.

After a snack and a snooze and as the credits roll through the end of a *Frasier* double bill, I'm startled by a dull thud on the patio door. Concerned initially, raising my head from the cushion and expecting to see a stunned bird lying concussed on the floor, I'm soon grinning as what I assume is a second shoe spinning over the wall to strike a second thud against the glass. Almost exactly one hour to the minute since Barry had accepted his task and it's mission complete: two shoes there on the balcony, home-coming heroes back from behind enemy lines. In my haste to get up I bang my knee hard against the coffee table, but the pain doesn't sour the moment or slow me down or stop me from calling out as the door slides open.

'You bloody beauty, Barry!'

When I reach the balcony wall and peer down, Barry isn't there. Nobody is. Movement in my periphery draws my eyes to the right, where a dishevelled figure is hauling himself up from the ground, using the back of the bench as leverage. Worryingly, it isn't the tramp, though, and as the man straightens and lifts his head my heart sinks. It's Barry, and from the way he is hobbling I know immediately that things have gone very wrong, that he's been kicked in the groin and, worst of all, he has no shoes on. A knot twists my stomach, tightens further as I turn around to see not my pristine, classic Adidas lying on the floor but a pair of shabby, very average Reeboks. Snap back round to Barry, now leaving the park and struggling towards me, still limping and holding his nose too, blood oozing through his fingers. He really is crap at fighting.

'Shit, what happened!'

'He's a nutter, Liam, I tell you. All I said was that my mate wants his trainers back and he flew at me. Headbutted me then kicked me in the nuts. I tell you, mate, you don't want to get involved, summat not right with him, pal. Can I have my shoes back?'

I toss his shoes down one at a time. Barry lowers himself tenderly, sits on the kerbside to put them on, but before he starts loosening the laces he places something on the pavement near to him.

'What's that, next to your right leg?'

Barry picks the object up again and presents it to me. 'This, you mean? It's my mask.'

It isn't a face mask. For a start, it isn't square and small, too big and too round. It isn't white or blue either. It has a picture on it. A picture of what looks to be an old man's face, a face that I kind of recognise, pretty sure that it's someone famous and… oh my god, it is a mask!

'A fuckin' Jeremy Corbyn mask! What the hell, Barry!'

'Yeah, well, you said to scare him, remember? Wear a mask, you said, and that's all I had, from that election night party that Geoff organised last year.'

'Think, Barry, think! Why on earth would I tell you to go and lean on someone dressed up as the leader of the Labour

Party, eh? I meant a face mask, to protect yourself against Covid, you barmy bugger! And why the hell would anyone would be scared of Jeremy Corbyn anyway! Unless they're Jewish, of course. Is he, Barry? Is the nasty beardy man on the bench Jewish? Did you offer him a bacon sandwich, just to check, before you tried to scare the crap out him by pretending to be a sixty-five-year-old anti-Semite?'

'Yeah, well, like I say, the mask was your idea. And he's your problem now, Liam, because I want nowt more to with it.'

Barry doesn't bother to finish tying his shoes. He gets up, rising through the pain that had lowered him down so gingerly, and as he stomps away I can't help thinking that he's more pissed at me than the tramp who not long ago had smashed his face in. Damn it, what a mess!

Or is it?

Let's think about this for a minute. The bench is still empty, with no sign of Lying Larry Smith anywhere to be seen, so even though the plan went spectacularly wrong, maybe things have worked out okay regardless, for me at least. Naturally I have to accept that the shoes are gone for good, but the main thing is that the tramp has gone with them! Yes, his leaving makes perfect sense! I'm pretty sure that vagrancy is against the law (if not, then it's certainly frowned upon), but the local coppers generally turn a blind eye to it, tolerate the homeless, but only on the understanding that they keep to their side of the bargain by not menacing anyone. This mother has done far more than simply get pissed and shout after people on a sunny afternoon; he's actually assaulted a member of the public, and in broad daylight too! Lying

Larry Smith must know that breaking the unspoken code like this makes his continued occupation of Woodlands Park untenable.

I check for him again, this time leaning outside of the balcony, shifting my weight until my centre of gravity is only a belt's width below the tipping point where I'd over-balance. Left, right, straight ahead; as far as I can see in any direction there is no sign of the tramp, and my relief slumps me back down into my chair.

'Seems I'm going to have to take this to another level, Liam. Both literally and figuratively.'

There is a dark energy in this voice, seemingly powerful enough to rise from the street and then echo back so that it sounds like it came from behind me. Deep down I know that this isn't possible, yet still I deny the physics, convince myself that my echo theory is correct because if it isn't then the voice could have come from only one place. My balcony, which is impossible, right?

A chill grips me, freezes me to the spot. I'm shaking, don't dare to turn to look.

'You do know that there will have to be consequences for what you did, don't you? I mean, come on, Liam, what the hell were you thinking, trying to intimidate me like that? I was only messing with you, fella, I'd have given you back your shoes eventually, but now you've gone and made it all serious. Why did you have to take the fun out of it, eh, get all *Sopranos* on me? Kudos on the mask idea, though. Had me worried there for a minute, enough to make me get in first anyway. Surprising how easily he went down for a big lad, though, don't you think?'

I'm dreading the words that I'm about to speak, but just as that morbid fascination forces you to watch car crash compilation shows, so too I have to know the grizzly details behind his threats, no matter how unpleasant they might be for me.

'What exactly do you mean, when you say consequences?'

My question is answered by bright, metallic clangs. He's moving! My legs tense, ready to launch. My left hand grasps a small glass ashtray that I'll sling at him then dash for the door, but when I turn, rather than being confronted by a bearded, lunging face, all I see is the back of the tramp's head descending from view beyond my balcony wall. He's on the fire escape! With the threat retreating I follow him, run to the wall in time to see him leap and bound down the last of the checker-plate steps, planting the ground with a sure-footed confidence that only a good pair of quality trainers can give you. Once there he walks away, not bothering to turn as he calls back to me.

'Game on, Liam, game on!'

9

'See that fire escape on the apartment block opposite? Do you reckon you could get across to one of the balconies from it?'

Matt thinks about this for a moment then puts his coffee down and stands clear of his table. He bends his knees repeatedly, shooting his arms forward each time he straightens up as if to complete the leap in his imagination. Next he paces along his balcony, stops and turns back to face me.

'I reckon, what, two, maybe two and a half metres max? So from here to the partition, yeah?'

Whilst he flexes and stretches I google, and the news isn't good. The world record for a standing jump is just short of three and a half metres so I'm thinking that even someone who is moderately athletic could probably make it. Matt proves my worst fear, leaps and in a single bound reaches the metal dividing bars, has to raise his hands to prevent his face from banging into them.

'Easy, mate, why d'you ask? You forgot how to open your door? I know it's been a while.'

'Yeah, summat like that. By the way, you jump like a girl.'

'You should know, mate. I'm thinking you've seen a lot of girls jump. Usually backward in horror when you get your kit off or more likely in front of a bus when you ask 'em out.'

I had intended to ask him if Jenny had mentioned anything about me, but the moment is ruined; I won't get a serious answer from Matt when he's in this mood. I let him take the last word with him back inside then walk to the end of my balcony to take another look at the gap, the only thing that stands between me and the tramp. With my arm held straight I can almost reach halfway to the fire escape without really trying. If anything it's less than two metres, not even far enough to stop the virus never mind leaping Larry. I need a plan, something to close this breach in my defences.

I wonder about relocating the metal partition that's between me and Matt, but that would need some serious tools and result in genuine damage to the building because, on closer inspection, those bars are set deep into the concrete at either end. The only other large anything that even closely resembles security bars is the wooden grill behind John's bed, and it's whilst checking behind there, to see what kind of fixings hold it in place, that I have a spark of inspiration. In truth, it was an actual spark that chastised my fiddling fingers when I grabbed a loose wire supplying his 'boudoir' bed lights. They may be low voltage but still carry enough juice to give me a belt sufficient to sit me back on my arse.

I hate these flashing lights, have done ever since John took them from last year's Christmas tree and wound them around the top of his headboard. Not because they are cheap and tacky and bright enough to spill a carpet of shifting colour onto the landing outside his door, but because apparently they work! Unbelievably I have met girls, half-dressed strangers in my kitchen wearing only knickers and a #metoo T-shirt, who have blamed not only drink but those 'oh-so-romantic lights' for betraying the feminist movement. #twinkletwinkleoopsmybra more like.

'Well, my shiny little friends, if you can put those slutty young tramps on their back for John, let's see what you can do for me with a beardy middle-aged one.'

The image that is set reeling through my head is disgusting to say the least and I regret saying these words out loud. Over and over I have to see the tramp naked, rolling on the bed, and he only stops his dirty, stinky seduction once I've finished untangling the string of lights and moved out of the bedroom to go collect the other things I need: a roll of duct tape and a pair of scissors from the kitchen cupboard.

Whether I am the Road Runner or Wile E Coyote remains to be seen, but with the components of my ACME tramp trap thrown into a shopping bag I'm ready to find out. I hook a mask over my ears, raise it onto my nose, check the straps a second time and then, for the first time in days, I open my front door.

It is spookily quiet in the corridor, drawing a sharp breath from me that sucks my face covering close and in doing so heightens the sense of danger in this place. Seeing the long, narrow passage abandoned like this is indeed very powerful, a snapshot of a metropolis ravaged by fear and death, but as unsettling as that is, it's the silence that really chills me because in normal times there is always noise here. There's a new normal now; the virus has seen to that. In a matter of days this thing has closed and bolted doors, isolated and clammed shut the trembling mouths that cower behind them as the world battens down to ride out what we are told is the first wave of a pandemic tha—

'Alright, Liam, want anything from the shops?'

Mr Higgs has stepped out from the flat two doors down. No mask, no gloves, no nothing.

'No, I don't as it happens, thank you very much! And I especially don't want a dose of the virus, if you don't mind, Derek!'

'Sorry, son, didn't quite catch that through your mask. Mumbling your words a bit too much for my old ears. Say again?'

I don't get the chance to articulate once more my disapproval because Margaret has heard us, opened her door to join us in the corridor and place an order.

'You off to the shops, Derek? Couldn't get me a meat pie from Greggs, could you, love? Janet, Alice, do you two want anything for lunch? Derek's off to the shops.'

Janet orders a sausage roll and Alice has a pasty. Neither of these people should be in my building. They are her friends, visiting from god knows where, but the one thing that I do know is that wherever they live no one bothers with masks or hand sanitiser. In that moment I realise that this virus doesn't have to be particularly sly or smart to move around; it just needs to be able to hold on to a hand or surf a droplet of moisture to hitch a ride on the next leg of its world tour. I get the feeling that these people would stop on a midnight road to pick up a blood-drenched loner if he had his thumb held out, help him load his chainsaw into the boot as they ask him where he's trying to get to. Idiots, all of them, and all I can do is shake my head.

'Oooo, you look like some sexy doctor or surgeon or something, Liam, very dapper, I must say. Hey, Alice, that boil on your foot still bothering you? Maybe Liam can sort you out. Get on the bed and I'll send him in to give you a little prick. And after, maybe he can lance that boil too!'

I don't know Alice and she doesn't know me, but she cackles raucously. I hate old women, especially those that, whenever they're sat with a couple of friends on a park bench or stood waiting at the bus stop, it's mandatory for them to make crude comments towards any sub-forty-year-old bloke who happens by.

'I'm not wearing this for a bloody joke, Margaret!'

'Really? Well, you look hilarious and very cute too, hun. Oh, if I was twenty years younger!'

'Yeah? Well, if you were twenty years younger, Margaret, you'd still be my granny!'

The cackling stops, the door slams and Derek scuttles on his way. Okay, I admit that was a tad nasty, but still, how come I'm the bad guy here?

Time to focus back on the job in hand, push hard on the bar that opens the fire door and step out on to the metal stairway. I feel good about my plan, for a moment at least until I realise with some dread that the view of the park from here is near as damn it the same as it is from my balcony. Sure enough, standing on the fire escape and looking back across at my chair I reckon that I could, with little effort, pretty much step on to my wall and seeing this I realise that the fairy light line of defence which I'm about to put in place is both my first and last.

I get to work, first stringing out the cable. Next, I insulate the handrail with duct tape at intervals of about a hand's width then strip corresponding sections of plastic coating from the lighting wire. These sections of bare copper I line up with the tape wrapped around the rail and fix them there, all the time visualising where someone might place their hands should they prepare to clamber over. Finally, I lean out and toss the plug across the gap, making sure that there is enough wire strung out behind it to reach inside the flat, then bundle up the remaining mass of lights into a tight ball which I leave tucked in the corner, out of sight behind a heavy stanchion.

Safely back inside the apartment and it's time to test. The plug clicks in to one of the power sockets in the lounge and thankfully the TV stays on! Good, nothing has shorted out, so there's no metal-on-metal contact. Out on to the balcony now to check that it's all working. Good, the lights are blinking, telling me that the circuit is complete and that the bare wires running across those patches of insulating tape are bristling with finger-tingling amps just waiting to shock anyone that grasps them. Only problem is that the bright ball of flashing colour is too conspicuous, even in daylight, so I go back inside and snip a small switch from John's bedside lamp. Connecting this into the circuit is tricky as the wires are very fine, so when it's done I rope both ends of the switch cover with duct tape. Last job is to re-route the cable along the wall, offer the switch up to the underside of the coffee table and use yet more tape to pin it there, out of the weather and out of view.

Job done, sat back down in my morning coffee spot, it's time to practise. I spend the next five minutes repeatedly placing my hand around an imaginary coffee cup on top of the table then reaching underneath to find and flick the switch, all the time watching the lights. Muscle memory builds quickly and when the lights go on for a fifth time in a row with no fumbling, I know I'm ready.

Game on indeed.

10

Normally one of the first things I do when I open my hotmail is go to my junk folder, 'select all' then 'empty folder'. Today, though, among the lonely Tatianas, the romantic Anastasias and the Russian fifteen-year-olds threatening to send videos of me watching porn to my mum unless I wire them Bitcoin, there is a message from ReginaldMullen@bt.co.uk. The subject line reads simply 'To Liam'. This has to be him.

Click.

Dear Liam,

My name is Reggie. I live in the apartment block opposite. You have called across to me on a number of occasions. Please accept my apologies for not replying. This is because I am recovering from an operation on my throat that makes it difficult for me to talk.

Yours sincerely,

Reggie

Initial excitement that my initiative has worked and that Reggie has got in touch is dampened by the apparent lack of information here. That said, when I read his words again I realise that actually his short note tells me a lot about Reginald Mullen. First and foremost, he is a proud man, someone who at the first opportunity finds it necessary to apologise for appearing rude, protective of his reputation. He is guarded too, offers no more details than absolutely necessary to explain his actions, but he also has a healthy outlook on life. There's no moaning about being shielded from the pandemic and neither does Reggie consider himself ill; he is recovering. Yes, he does tell me that it's difficult for him to talk, but there's no sympathy sought, no mention of the pain that he must be in. Yeah, I like Reggie a lot.

> Hi Reggie, great to hear from you. Let me know if you need anything. It would be good to keep in touch and maybe meet up for a pint when this is over. See you on the balcony! Take care. Liam

I reckon it's going to take a little while longer to get to know the old fella well enough to ask him about his gun, but I will. I'm still considering how to manipulate our next exchange towards this goal when Mum's profile picture pops onto the screen. I accept the call but when the video starts the settee is empty. Well, almost empty: I can see Mum's arm and the back part of her head, and I start to laugh, am about to tell her to move into frame when I hear my dad's voice, loud but controlled, not quite a shout.

'…like I've told you before. Yes, she's important to me, Brenda! You know that, so why do we have to have this conversation time and time again!'

'Because I need you here, Billy! This isn't what we agreed! You promised me that you'd be here for me, that we could make this work, but it isn't, it's all about you and what you need, isn't it, so why don't you just fuck off back to your holiday home then!'

Mum is shouting and swearing, a rare, terrifying event that forces Dad's voice louder to match it.

'How many times do I have to tell you, Brenda, it's a shed!'

I slap the laptop closed, cut the accidental call. What the hell was that about?! I know what I heard: far too much and with nowhere near enough ambiguity for me to pretend that this isn't bad, very bad indeed. Shit! None of this is going to make any sense without scotch. On my way to the balcony I twist the top from a bottle of Johnny Walkers and don't feel the slightest bit guilty as I pour myself a large one under the disapproving glare of a sun that hasn't yet dipped behind the city skyline.

Shot one. So let's break this down. My dad is having an affair, that's a fact. Okay, okay, not good, but don't panic. After all, as unpleasant as this is, he's a bloke, and blokes do that kind of stuff. It isn't for me to get in the middle of what's going on between them. They're an adult couple and it's for them to sort out. They'll be fine.

Shot two. But Mum's attitude? It makes no sense, totally bizarre! She obviously knows about the affair. This isn't what we agreed, she'd said. Agreed? Yes, my dad can be a straight talker, humourless bastard too, but is he really capable of being so bloody cold? Brenda, darling, I have something to tell you. With your agreement I'm going to take a lover. Okay, Billy, love, grab a calendar and let's work out a timetable. No, this bit just doesn't make any sense.

Shot three. This is bullshit! No one agrees to share their partner after thirty-odd years, not in the real world. That shit's for US trailer-trash documentaries or struggling soaps trying to shock their viewing figures back to life. It is not my mum! It is not my dad. But it is, isn't it, can't deny what they both said, and then even when Mum's pouring her heart out, all he's bothered about is that she forgot to call the shed a bloody shed! Not a word about how much he's hurt her! Arsehole.

Shot four. Well, no more, I'm going to tell him what I bleedin' think, that's what. He can't treat my mum like this, pissing her around with her feelings an' all that as if she just has to take his shit, like she can't survive without him. Ooo, look at me, Billy big balls who can just walk over anyone whenever I like and don't give a toss if they get hurt – well, I say no, Billy Slater, no more! I'm not havin' it and if my mum's not got the guts enough to stand up to you then I bleedin' will. No way, no how, I'm not having it!

Shot five. What d'you think, Mr Bucket Head? Is my dad a knobhead or what?

True, I am very drunk, but I'm not seeing things. Well, obviously, I am seeing things, admittedly a little blurred too, but the object sliding through my view is definitely a real thing, not a hallucination. Unable to properly process what I am looking at, all I can do is to rest my cheek on the cool table top and watch it pass: a pink bucket with a smiley face drawn on it, swinging gently from a rope as it is lowered down from somewhere above to somewhere below.

'Night night, Mr Bucket Head.'

Game over.

11

My head is battered and banging. The whiteboard is screaming at me.

DAD IS A TWAT!!!!!

I groan, remember why I'd felt it so important to struggle and sway, support the wall with one hand and scrawl these words on my way to collapse into bed. Poor Mum.

I need water, and I need it fast – I dash to stick my head under the bathroom tap, but the air I suck in along with the glugs and slurps immediately forces my head back up. Impossible to suppress, violent coughs then snort water and something else all over the zombie in the mirror. Shit, I look terrible, and I'm thinking seriously of going straight back to bed when above my left shoulder I see in the reflection that there's a weird little sketch on the board. Why would I draw SpongeBob SquarePants? And why is there a stick protruding from his flat-top head, as though he's been in a spear-fishing accident? It takes a moment to decipher the mirror writing beneath it and reveal the answer.

'Oh yeah, there was a bucket! Mr Bucket Head! What the hell was that about?'

I reckon I must have made this drawing so that I wouldn't dismiss as a booze-fuelled dream any hazy flashback of seeing that bucket swinging in front of my balcony. Not that I think this is important, or at least I can't imagine it being so, but Mr Bucket Head is certainly intriguing and something to puzzle about.

A strange noise drifts to me from the lounge: a rapid slapping sound bouncing down the hallway. Once satisfied that this isn't the sound of neurons popping in my ailing head, I dry my face and walk towards it. In the lounge the TV is off. The patio door is open but there's no breeze to rustle blinds so the source of the noise remains a mystery until a distant shout arrives with it: god bless you or something like that. It's coming from outside.

When I walk out onto the balcony I can see that the noise has enticed Reggie onto his too. He is standing stiffly, holding a military salute which he only lowers briefly so that he can wave back at me. In the other hand he is holding that gun, pressed tightly to his side. The noise is louder now and the more I look around the more people I can count, a hundred at least standing on their balconies: some clapping, some waving signs decorated with rainbows and calling down simple thank-you messages to the street below.

'I thought this was happening tomorrow Reggie, this clapping for carers thing?'

Not sure why I would ask such an open question to a

mute man, but bless him, Reggie does his best to oblige me. He first shrugs his shoulders (confirming that he too has a mix-up with the days) then points along the road, towards the main high street where I can see an explanation for this appreciative, mass outpouring.

A nurse approaches. She is a solitary figure, slowly but purposefully making her way down the middle of the street. The image of this tiny woman walking in to battle on my behalf is powerful indeed and it slaps my hands together so furiously that they hurt, but I don't care. I want to feel this pain, feel something physical to keep me mindful of this almost spiritual moment shared with someone whose bravery is surpassed only by the humility that holds her head down. It's as if she is embarrassed, not worthy to receive this gratitude, but believe me, girl, oh boy do you deserve this! I bet that, if I were to ask, you would tell me with a sincere smile that you're 'just doing your job'.

But it isn't just a job; it takes so much more than a sense of duty to walk this way when everyone around you is turning to run in the opposite direction, to hide and hope that you win.

Someone further down, a couple of floors up in the block opposite, wolf whistles. Bit inappropriate, this, but I can kind of understand why they would. The nurse's skirt is very short and each solemn step causes it to ride up her thigh a little, revealing the tell-tale black stripe of a suspender belt. The girl can't resist looking up towards the whistling man and when she does her playfully scolding face reminds me of someone, looks a bit like Penny, the hot one, though, from an episode of *Big Bang Theory*, when… hang on a minute!

'Hey, Jenny! Is that you? Jesus, girl, I must admit, you make one hell of a sexy nurse!'

A voice from above slams down on to me. 'So what you saying, eh? Just because she's a woman she can't look nice when she goes to work? She's a hero, you sexist pig! Grow up!'

'Oh no, you've got me all wrong. She's not a real nurse, she's just going to a fancy-dress party at my mates.'

The minute that I hear my words echoing down the road I realise what I've done, but it's too late. In my haste to protect my reputation I've exposed hers to ridicule. I've pushed the plunger, like in one of those demolition videos, and as the news of this deception ripples through the apartment complex so each pillar of public support for her is sequentially blown to bits. Eventually there is nothing left to hold her pedestal high and it collapses around her: claps turn to boos, insults rain down and Jenny can't run from it quickly enough. When she is almost directly below me, she does slow her stride, but only enough such that she can be sure I'll hear her call up.

'Way to go, Lidl! I was actually wearing this outfit as a little tease for you, but you can kiss that goodbye!'

Jenny flips a finger and disappears from sight, off to join the other doctors and nurses gathered at Matt's Covid party to self-medicate her anger with vodka until she is feeling well enough again to join the discussions about how pleasing it is to see that the transmission rate of memes, jokes and GIFs is finally falling.

For me it's a closed patio door and time alone to reflect. I've always thought of myself as being a pretty chilled kind of guy, never allowing those trivial yet irritating annoyances to get under my skin, but this series of events (the trainers and the tramp, Mum and Dad, and now a fit girl slipping through my fingers) – well, to be honest I can sense an unsettling frustration building. Don't get me wrong, I'm still of the opinion that talking to someone about my personal problems isn't necessary to help me resolve them, but that said, I could really do with talking to anyone about anything else to take my mind off it all.

Trouble is there's no one available at the moment. I'm not ready to face Mum and Dad yet – still too raw, that. John is at the party next door, already fully briefed on something he already knows: that his flatmate is a self-righteous prick who doesn't know when to shut his mouth. The balcony's out of bounds too, of course, so yeah, good job well done, Liam, enjoy the rest of your hangover!

I'm wallowing in self-pity when my laptop dings to tell me that it has an email for me. It's from Reggie and I'm immediately lifted.

Dear Liam,
It is often hard to do the right thing. Do not be discouraged.
Yours sincerely,
Reggie

Top bloke, this. How such a simple message can be so meaningful impresses me, puts me in awe of Reggie and the way that he makes every word count with no need for the fluff that I know I often revert to. As I write my reply I keep this lesson in mind, try and emulate his example. Three or four minutes into the process and it strikes me how difficult it actually is to distil a thought down to its fundamentals. When I do finish tweaking and deleting the result is pleasing, gives me confidence that putting that bit of extra effort in was worth it and has made the expression of my gratitude so much more.

Thank you, Reggie.

Send.

12

The morning is a lot brighter. My head is clear and so are my thoughts. The tramp isn't on the bench; no contact with him since he assaulted Barry and stormed the fire escape, so perhaps the police have moved him on after all. I did see Jenny earlier, draped around Matt as they shared breakfast. She looked happy, him not so much because it turns out that morning Jenny talks a lot, mainly crap. I couldn't help but overhear a large amount of her incessant drivel, but I had to put my noise-cancelling ear buds in when she complained to Matt about how her brother, a career thief, is struggling to find empty houses to rob during the lockdown. A far bigger turn-off for me, though, the thing that made me feel completely okay about losing her last night, was that morning Jenny looks nothing like hot Penny. Yep, I definitely dodged a bullet there and the thought of Matt spending the next few awkward weeks at work trying to unravel himself from a horrible blonde mistake really cheers me up. As for Mum and Dad, well, I have come down firmly on the side of not my business. I will call today and I will be wary of Mum's mood, but the fact is that, had I not overheard their argument, I would never have suspected anything was wrong so, on the whole, they must be dealing okay with their situation.

Good, all is good and not a single problem shared. In your face morning television chat shows! In fact, I'm feeling so pleased with myself that I think it's time to clear another obstacle. I need milk, the shop isn't too far and the streets are quiet, so sod it, I'm going out. Wonder if Reggie needs anything.

Hi Reggie, I'm off to the shops. Need anything?

Reggie answers quickly, faster than most of my dumbass mates can direct message.

Dear Liam,
Thank you but I have everything I need.
Yours sincerely,
Reggie

Taking the fire escape to the ground kills two birds with one stone. Not only do I avoid the lift (which is basically a big metal petri dish with buttons) but it also gives me the opportunity to check out the wiring on the tramp trap. It's intact, something that can't be said about the missing metal grill door that should be in place to close off public access to the bottom step. I make a mental note to let the building services manager know about this, not that it will be fixed anytime soon.

Stepping out onto the street is a lot less stressful than I had imagined. There is no one about, so I lower my mask. It's a mistake because the moment that I do this, I'm recognised.

'Hey, look who it is, it's that moron who was slagging the nurse off. Tosser!'

I don't have the energy to explain yet again why I had protested last night's clapping, so I crack on at a brisk pace. On the plus side, there aren't too many people who answer the man's rallying call, but unfortunately, those that do are spread out along the balconies meaning that for pretty much the full length of the apartment complex I am subjected to boos and insults. I don't know these people, recognise none of their voices, so I'm stunned and left wondering who the hell Matt has been gossiping with when one of them calls out my new nickname: limp dick Liam. I do have a smile to myself, though, when another woman shouts down that she too has been a very, very naughty nurse and she needs to be punished. It's hard not to glance up, to see if there's any merit in answering her, but I manage to resist.

Hitting the high street, it's time to put my mask on properly as there are a few more people here. Covering my nose and mouth in this way attracts far more head shakes from the non-believers than it does reassuring nods from fellow maskees but I'm pleased to be in the minority, especially so as I stride smugly towards a teenager, no older than fourteen, who has been halted outside the shop by a sign mandating that masks must be worn. There is another sign too explaining that if you ring the bell then one of the shop assistants will arrive with a mask but that this service will cost you five pounds. It seems a little steep, to be honest, and I can understand why the lad is swearing so loudly, but hey ho, I've got mine.

'Here, mate, can I borrow your mask?'

The kid is serious too, his insane request summing up perfectly how mistaken our leader's reliance on 'good old common sense' to beat this virus really is. I ask the lad to move away from the door, demand my right to social distance and he shuffles along but can't resist calling me a 'scaredy twat'. More evidence, if any were needed, that some people just don't get it.

Mr Shan gets it. He's taken the trouble to put yellow tape on the floor so that the limited number of people he allows into his Spa can shop there safely. I follow a man and his toddler around the store's one-way system. They are taking a hellishly long time to choose what to have for tea, but unlike a week or two ago, I don't for one minute resent them for it. Take your time – I actually say these words and mean them too because one thing that this pandemic has removed (along with the old and the infirm) is the structure from our lives, the need to rush through it. So, despite the slow pace, there is no frustration and I arrive at the till clutching two pints of milk, fresh from the fridge and as chilled as my demeanour.

'That'll be four pound twenty, please, sir.'

'Are you having a laugh? Over two quid for a pint of milk?'

'It's called supply and demand, sir.'

'Supply! You've got loads of bleedin' milk! I've just seen it! So where exactly is the supply problem?'

'Well, if you don't like it, you could always go and shop at… Lidl.'

How many people has Matt told! I tap my card on his pay machine as angrily as I can and step away, leaving my good mood and one of the milk cartons by the till. At the door I turn back, vow never to step foot in his shop again and Mr Shan tells me good, that he doesn't want my kind of customers anyway. When pressed as to what the hell he means by that, he widens his eyes and points to a 'Thank you NHS' rainbow poster sellotaped on the wall.

'You should be ashamed about what you said to that nurse.'

'Yeah? Well, you should be ashamed, about what you're doing to milk.'

I know it's a terrible comeback, makes no sense whatsoever, but I am flustered and angry and desperate to have the last word. Still, there is no excuse for it. I'm disgusted with myself, simply nothing worse than a weak retort and this one was particularly bad. It deserves the disapproving, head-shaking tutting of the teenager who's still waiting outside.

'Man, that was weak.'

I remove my mask and offer it to him. 'Here, on condition that you nick as much as you can from that robbing bastard. Deal?'

Unlike Fagin, I do have reservations about the crime I'm commissioning and I wince a little as my freshly groomed, child-sized shoplifter slides the mask over his grinning promise, gives me a thumbs-up. I know I've done a bad thing, but there again, I also know that Mr Scam deserves to have his racketeering punished, so go, go and fill your boots, little one, use those sticky little fingers to pick his profits.

Having no plausible deniability should this go tits-up and the police get involved, I don't hang around, cross back over the road and walk quickly towards Paradise Heights. Turning off the high street and once out of sight, I feel safe enough to slow down but then have to stop completely when a loud, brash cry from above announces my return. I can't be bothered to walk the gauntlet again so I turn around, take a right at the main road this time and scuttle along it, staying tight to the buildings. It's not far to the next junction and once I've strolled casually past a couple of houses, halfway along Oak Terrace, I relax, re-evaluate my route home.

To get back to my flat from here wouldn't be difficult as there are plenty of ginnels offering me shortcuts that will keep me from bumping into people. These narrow alleys cut through backyards, enable binmen to empty the trash and breezes to purge the stench of dog poo, often blended with their drunken owner's urine. There is a light wind today, but nevertheless, this is the scent that hits me, carries me back to the ginnel where I once learned to ride a bike and where I kissed my first girl.

I have an idea.

Mum's house is less than a ten-minute walk from here. I'm already out and about, could do with the exercise and the back streets are all but deserted, so why not? On the other hand, I don't fully understand the why either. After all, there is no guarantee that Dad will be there, but as conflicted as I am, I can't shake the urge to go and stand on one of those bins, peek over the wall, look down through a high window and see him in his shed. I have no idea as to what I'd say to him if he were to catch me peeking in, but my inability to answer these questions doesn't stop my legs from taking me there. As it happens, on entering the alley behind Warren Street, right away the first unknown is resolved for protruding above the red-brick wall at the back of Mum's house is a narrow slice of shed window and the light is on.

'He's in.'

In order to answer my second question, however, I will need a wheelie bin, so having checked for passers-by and nosey neighbours, I drag one from across the alley to position it next to the wall. I check again to be sure that the rattling hasn't roused any interest. It hasn't, so it's time to reach up, grab the top of the wall and clamber on to the bin, mumbling as I go that if I am spotted then I can just say hi. Nothing weird about that; he's my dad.

Slowly I lift my head above the wall.

Other than Dad, there are a number of things that I could reasonably have expected to see through that dusty window. Granted, some of the options are more likely than others. Mum could have been there, for example, taking her turn to be alone and making the point that it's her shed too. An empty room would also have made sense, Dad having left the light on whilst he nips back to the house to use the loo. Who knows, perhaps something other than people could have turned it on. Would it be such a stretch for an inquisitive rat to be caught red-pawed, sniffing at a switch that he's flicked on accidentally when stretching to see if there's anything tasty on the shelf next to i?. Any of these possibilities would have been better, any of them more palatable than the woman that I'm looking at standing in Dad's shed, waiting patiently for her lover to arrive.

It's a real gut punch, this, drops me back down to crouch on the top of the bin with my back to the wall, with my back to her. What a bitch! I mean, how brazen a hussy do you have to be to put on your best dress, walk in broad daylight and high heels down a grimy alley then sneak through a gate left open by a man who is sat with his wife only metres away? And what kind of man could do this?! Drink tea, pass pleasantries with my mum, all the time keeping one eye on the TV and the other on the shed light, waiting for the signal that his booty call has arrived!

I'd only had enough stomach to snatch a glance, but the image of the other woman is scorched onto my mind. In a weird way too, I feel like I'm also being unfaithful to Mum because underneath my angry disgust there's an unsavoury admission that my dad's bit on the side is very attractive, her party dress hugging a figure that any thirty-year-old would die for. Damn it, Dad, why not some old slapper?! At least give my mum a fighting chance!

I double down on my resolution that ultimately this has nothing to do with me. My struggle to get my head around the complexity of their relationship isn't what matters here. What is important is Mum and how she is, so stick to the plan. Be aware and be ready to help pick up the pieces should the load become unbearable, should his infidelity break their marriage. And try not to judge Dad either. Oh, and above all else, definitely try to stop thinking about how much you'd like to see the face that owns that kick-ass body!

13

My head is in bits as I leave the alley, still processing the images glimpsed in the shed. Luckily, I don't need brainpower to get home, to decide the lefts and the rights or the cross heres. I grew up on these streets and so it's autopilot that eventually lands me at the entrance to Woodlands Park. This isn't the gate that I can see from my balcony, though, which is basically nothing more than a break in the hedge. No, I'm at the Westgate Entrance, one of two main portals to the park, both of which are flanked with heavy cast-iron gates that used to be part of a ring of fenced steel fully enclosing the park. Control of the gates was the job of the park keeper way back when and it would be his job to close them diligently every evening, according to the schedule written in large gold letters on a big green board set at the entrance. These days, although the green board remains, the fence is gone and the gates are chained open. Can't be sure why but I think it was the local police who insisted on this, the idea being to tip the balance, give easy access to police cars should podgy PCs need to chase into the dark park any dodgy dealers who've been set running by flashing blue lights. Those gates used to tower above me and my mates, unscalable if we ever wanted to get onto the footy pitch after hours for a late kickabout. More daunting back then, however, had been getting trapped inside the park, on the few occasions that we'd lost track of Mum's curfew. Escape then required an act of bravery unparalleled in a nine-year-old's world: a knock on the door of the parky's hut.

Parky Joe was basically my childhood bogeyman and I get chills even now remembering those times, stood crapping myself at his hut door whilst my mates hid in the bushes, left me alone and wondering if I'd be the next kid to get dragged inside. One of my pals' dad worked for the police and Jimmy swore on his brother's life that he'd heard his parents talking about some orphanage in Liverpool where at least five missing local kids had been found, muted by the horror they'd endured. Each of them had been snatched from the park and each of them was only able to communicate using a pen and pad. The sketches that they scrawled had all been the same: terrifying images from the inside of Parky Joe's hut and the three-barred electric fire there that he'd used to roast them into silence before smuggling them away. All bullshit, of course, but looking back I reckon that the kids relished this story and the fear it brought them. I wouldn't be surprised if Parky Joe hadn't enjoyed his notoriety too on some level.

These days there's a new bogeyman in the park, and as I swing around a majestic rhododendron bush I see that he's back, sitting on his bench at the far end of the path that leads to my flat. I have a choice: be a man, stride confidently towards him and show this piece of shit that I'm not scared or be that frightened little boy again and sneak around the full perimeter of the park. As I do in all situations that have the potential for conflict I take the path of least resistance: the long way round. This is such a natural decision for me that there is zero self-recrimination as I weave through the trees in the opposite direction to where my nemesis sits. On the contrary I'm feeling pretty pleased with myself. Until I see him, that is: an old man sporting a banded fedora, hands tucked into the pockets of his tweed jacket, standing stock still halfway along a footpath cutting diagonally across the square of grass that I'm skulking around. I know who it is but can't confirm until I step out from under the shade of the trees and allow my eyes to adjust to the daylight.

'Granddad?'

No response. Maybe it isn't him.

'Norman! Norman Wallace!'

Hearing this name called snaps Granddad from out of his stupor and he turns towards me, takes a step in my direction. I dash to meet him, stopping a safe distance short but hopefully close enough to be recognised.

'What are you doing here, Granddad? Shouldn't you be in your home?'

I don't think he knows who I am.

'It's me, Liam. Your grandson.'

There's nothing registering, no glad surprise in his expression, just a deepening frown as he begins a slow turn away from me.

'I'm Brenda's son, Granddad. You remember Brenda, don't you?'

Finally, a memory flashes in, widens his eyes and opens his mouth.

'Ah, Brenda! Of course. How is my little girl? Is she with you, Billy?'

I need him to trust me. I need to get him back home, away from people and any potential contact with the virus, so rather than correcting him I reckon this will go a lot faster if I let him think that I am Dad.

'She isn't here, Norman, no. She's at the shops. Listen, why don't we go and have a cup of tea at your place, eh?'

I offer my hand and he moves towards it. I retreat, but not too far, and Granddad keeps a steady pace, trying to catch up with me. Like this we shuffle along the path until we are in shouting distance of the blue gate.

'Hey, you! I've got one of your residents here!'

Two men dressed in grubby white topcoats, both wearing protective masks, hurry to collect their charge, and as they familiarise Granddad with what is happening, I can't resist having a dig.

'Really, lads? Now, I'm no expert in geriatric care but I'm thinking that quite a big part of it would be to count how many old dudes you've got in the morning and then try and keep that number fairly constant during the day?'

They ignore me completely, gently grab an elbow either side and lead my Granddad away, back through the blue gate.

'Hey, Granddad, I'll come and see you when this is all over, I promise.'

Granddad doesn't say goodbye to me, too busy chatting with his carers, who he seems to be very comfortable with, and for a moment I feel bad about taking such a cheap shot at them, but this regret swiftly turns to anger at their neglect.

'And you two, get that bloody gate fixed! And take good care of my granddad!'

'So that's your granddad, is it?'

Whilst I've been distracted my bogeyman's crept up behind me, worryingly near enough to whisper in my ear with barely disguised evil pleasure at this snippet of information. Chilling, his voice is, and normally I'd run, but hearing mention of my granddad forces me to break the habit of a lifetime, spins me around and although he is far too close I am not backing away, not this time.

'You stay away from him, d'you hear! He has nothing to do with whatever problem you've got with me, right?'

The tramp smiles. 'Wrong actually, Liam, 'cos like I told you, the moment you sent your boy round to sort me out then all bets were off. But hey, I may be capable of a lot of things, but giving old people a good slapping isn't one of 'em.'

Two thoughts spring to mind. Firstly, why the hell would he mention beating up my granddad like that? Shit, I'd never even considered this as a possibility! All I'm asking is that he stays clear, keeps Granddad free of infection. And secondly, what age would have been the cut-off for violence here? Is a fifty-nine-year-old fair game should they accidentally bump him at the bar, spill his drink? Or sixty-four, perhaps? Dare to cut in front of me at the post office, would ya? Well, I'm sorry, pal, but as you don't have a bus pass, you're having it.

Barry had been spot on in his appraisal of this man; he is indeed dangerous and I regret standing my ground because having such a peek into the tramp's mind isn't going to help me sleep tonight. Time to be less of a hero and more of a Liam, so I try to reason with him.

'Look, all I'm asking is please just keep away from him, yeah?! He's old and this Covid thing is really dangerous for him.'

The tramp grins. 'Shit, Liam, chill out! You really are taking all this virus bollocks far too seriously, you know. You need to lighten up, have a bit of fun. Hey, here's a thought! Do you like gameshows?'

So random is this that I don't know what to say, so I shrug, hoping my indifference will end the exchange. It doesn't.

''Cos I've just come up with an absolute belter of an idea for one. *Who Wants to Lick an Octogenarian*, it's called, or summat like that. Needs a bit of work, but you get the idea.'

I really don't.

'So it works like this. Good ol' Granpappy Norman is out on one of his walkabouts and I go over and ask him a question. Now, if he gets the answer right then I go back to my bench and that's the end of it, but if he gets it wrong then that starts the clock. You with me so far, Liam? 'Cos this is where you come in. You see, once the timer starts I'll shout something like, "Liam Slater, come on down," and then you've got sixty seconds to come and join us! Cool, eh? But, and here's the kicker, if you don't manage to get to us before time's up then I lick your granddad, right on the lips. What d'you think? You up for it?'

No! For fuck's sake, no, I am not up for it! Jesus, what the hell is happening here?!

'Not too sure about it, Liam? Well, look, let me make it easier for you. You're playing!'

The tramp holds his arms and eyes wide open, licks his grubby lips slowly.

'Hmmmm, can almost taste those tea stains and biscuit crumbs! Yummy!'

Is he being serious here? Shit, I have no way of telling, but based on his behaviour so far, he does seem to be someone who can follow through on a threat, no matter how messed up that may be. Perhaps if I play along, indulge him a little then I can call his bluff, show him that I'm not convinced he'll follow through or even be bothered if he does? Yes, I need to diffuse his attempt to get inside my head.

'Oh, I'm up for it alright, just a bit hazy on some of the details, that's all. For one thing, the question you'll ask Granddad, would it be a multiple choice? Only fair, don't you think, give the daft old sod half a chance, right?'

The tramp thinks about this for a moment. 'Yeah, I think that would probably work, but I'd have to have another question ready for you, though. Too easy otherwise, if you just get a fifty-fifty shot.'

'My question? Erm, just remind me again, why would I be answering a question?'

The tramp coughs violently, no doubt to remind me what is at stake here. 'Ah, well, this is where it gets interesting, Liam. Now, I'm kind of making this up as we go along here, but I'm thinking that if you were to get to me and Norm before the two minutes is up then you could get a choice. Let's say that you can either answer a question or, or maybe cash out or... hey, I know! Something called "take one for the team"!'

I am actually kind of intrigued now. 'Go on.'

'Okay, so let's say you choose to answer a question, then that's a straight-forward double-or-nothing deal. By that I mean that if you get it right then you take Granddad home, but if you get it wrong then I lick you both. Now, the cash-out option's gonna be a simple exchange. Hey, how about a grand for Granddad, yeah! Shit, Liam, you gotta admit, I am on fire! Finally, and here's the one I'll be rooting for, if you choose to "take one for the team" then you have to stand there, hands behind your back, while I smash you in the face three times.'

The tramp laughs, eyes even wider now as he flips back to manic and menacing and whatever weird little world he'd lured me into vanishes, dumps me back to my awful reality in which I have a dangerous, cunning enemy who is serious about extortion, violence or licking my granddad. My strategy to take the heat out of this situation is in tatters and it's obvious now that through all this charade he was more than one step ahead of me. I need a rethink.

'You're a friggin' lunatic, pal. You really need to get help.'

I'm physically shaking as I walk away. For a while the tramp follows me, singing the theme tune to his bloody gameshow. It isn't until I am back through the gap in the hedge that he drops away and I can no longer hear him. What I do hear, though, as I walk through the shrubs, is a scraping and knocking sound above my head. When I look up I see a bucket suspended, swinging gently in a light breeze and bouncing off Mrs Wilson's balcony. She is reaching out to grab the rope, steadies it and then dips a bony hand inside Mr Bucket Head.

'Hi, Mrs Wilson, how are you doing? And if you don't mind me asking, what are you doing?'

'Oh, hello, Liam, love. Just getting my surprise. Now, what do we have today? Oh, how lovely, a chocolate bar!'

Mrs Wilson tugs the rope, shouts thank you as loudly as her frail voice allows and the bucket begins to rise back to where it came from: the fourth-floor balcony directly above mine. I can't see who is doing the hoisting, just the occasional hand reaching over the wall to grab and pull. The hand definitely belongs to a girl.

'Hey, that's a nice thing you're doing!'

No reply, no face peers down from above. Mr Bucket Head does halt his ascent though, jiggles about a little in thanks for the recognition of his charitable work and then continues on his way.

14

On balance I didn't much enjoy my sortie into the new norm outside of the flat, so it's with some trepidation that I open Reggie's email titled 'Can you help?'. I needn't have been concerned about him asking for a favour that might require me to go back out.

Dear Liam,

As I have committed not to open my door until the current situation is resolved I do not expect you to either. However, whilst I have sufficient rice, tinned meat and beans for approximately sixteen weeks, I am in need of a replacement charging box for my laptop computer. Can you help? The laptop computer is made by Hewlett-Packard, serial number 5ES85EA. Regarding delivery of the new charging box, I have attached a picture illustrating a method used by the navy for ship-to-ship transfers and which I propose may enable you to send the replacement between our buildings and also allow me to return payment without compromising our safety. What do you think of my idea?

Yours sincerely,

Reginald

What do I think? Reggie is suggesting that I somehow rig a line across the twenty-metre gap that separates our balconies and then use it to transport a very fragile piece of electrical equipment across to him, sixty feet above the road? I love it! I think it's a fantastically ridiculous idea, exactly the kind of distraction I need right now.

The picture that Reggie has sent me is a scanned copy of a grainy old photograph. There are two what look to be navy vessels steaming hard and perilously close, crashing through each other's wakes. Stretching between the ships there is a slack wire and suspended halfway along that is a cargo net filled with bundles of supplies. It's almost dipping into the water. At each end of the line there are four sailors and whilst I can't tell which from the photo, one team is pulling the supplies, the other feeding out a haul line for the return. I wonder if one of these young lads is Reggie.

Hi Reggie and yes, I think this is a great idea. I accept the mission! My flatmate has a charger that will work fine and I'm sure he will be happy for you to borrow it. As for the transfer line – well, I love a challenge! Give me a couple of days to get the things I need and I'll be in touch. I'll check in now and again from the balcony so if your battery empties before I get the charger to you then you'll just have to use signs and semaphore!

It doesn't take long to fill my Amazon basket with the necessary items. Once the order confirmations are received, I close down and go to check if Reggie is on his balcony so that I can tell him that, subject to the postman delivering on the seller's promise, Operation Highwire is a go for next Tuesday. He is there, waiting patiently for news and I call across to tell him my plan. Reggie takes a marker pen and writes a big 'OK' on a piece of paper, holds it high for me to read. It's a test, a check that he is writing things large enough to be seen from my balcony, ready for when the battery finally drains. I shout across to tell him that the font size is fine and then with a thumbs-up he disappears back inside to prepare his bean and corned beef dinner.

'What's with you and the old guy then, Liam? You finally given up on girls since Jenny told you to do one? Finally accepted that your future lies with someone a bit more wrinkly, a tad more penis-y?'

A shrill voice from inside Matt's flat blasts onto his balcony, demands to know what he is doing and how long he will be doing it for. Matt answers it with a chirpy, 'Not long, babe.'

'And how's that working out for you, Matt?

Matt turns to me, his face broken and desperate, no sign of his trademark cheeky-chappy grin, and I can't help laugh a little.

'It's not funny, Liam. She won't leave! Why won't she leave? She's put things in the bathroom mate, lady things.'

To a young, red-blooded male these words are as chilling as anything that the tramp could say. Which reminds me.

'Bit random, this, but let's say that you had a choice to be either punched in the face or have your granddad licked on the lips by a stranger. And let's assume it's someone who's got the virus. What would you choose?'

'For Christ's sake, what is it with you and old people?! Why the hell are you licking them? You're messed up, mate.'

'No, you bloody idiot, I'm not licking them, some other dude is.'

'What, and you're just watching? Hiding in the cupboard with your kecks round your ankles? You really need to get out more.'

I'm about to give up, understanding that this question is probably far too weird,(especially when you're sober), when Matt gives me his answer.

'Have to be the punch, I reckon. A broken nose'd be all fixed up in a week or so, but who knows what would happen if your granddad got it? Yeah, definitely. Punch in the face.'

Not that I believe this to be a choice that I will ever have to make, but it's good to have my conclusion confirmed. A dog-whistle voice, even more shrill and impatient than that a moment ago, calls Matt to heel, demands that breakfast be prepared, and like the gutless puppy he is he runs to it, tail wagging, leaving me to enjoy some peace and quiet on the balcony.

15

Over the next few days me and Reggie finalise the details of Operation Highwire. We spend at least a couple of hours each day working up a list of materials, based on the various sketches and ideas that we exchange. It's a welcome distraction for me from a nagging anxiety that's not quite tangible enough to keep me up at night but does churn my stomach periodically, should my mind be freed to wander.

Reggie's laptop does run out as expected but thankfully not before we have agreed the 'devil in the detail'. Good job too because it turns out that the natural fibre rope I had ordered wasn't to Reggie's liking: too fibrous, too likely to grab and snag the wheel of the castor under which the cargo will hang. Luckily I was able to modify the order, swap it out for a lighter-gauge synthetic cord before my package was dispatched. So, Tuesday held good for the charger transfer as long as the wind doesn't blow above a very specific twelve knots, whatever that is. This 'go, no-go' test is put in place at Reggie's insistence, based on some 'very hairy' first-hand experience from his navy days.

It turns out that midshipman Reginald Mullen was indeed in the photograph of the ship-to-ship cargo transfer that he'd sent me earlier. When challenged to pick him out I had to concede defeat pretty quickly as the bright white sailors on deck all look the same: wiry teens with cropped, jet-black hair. Even when Reggie pointed out that he was the third person in a line of men pulling supplies across to HMS *Bangor* (the minesweeper on which he served) the fifty feet between us today and a gap of seventy-five years proved far too much for me to connect his two faces. HMS *Bangor* was also where Reggie had been given the gun I'd seen on his balcony wall, the name of his ship scorched into the shoulder stock by crewmates who had awarded it to him for a selfless act but about which he would say little more, other than that it had also earned him medals.

Reggie's mission during the war had been to trawl explosive mines from the North Atlantic shipping routes and I guess that's where he developed a, well, let's say rather conservative sense of humour, dark enough to black out the horror that he witnessed. I think it's a bit rich that these days, in spite of his bravery and sacrifice, we don't allow Reggie to express those 1940s working-class values anymore, his right to do that having been a casualty of the war he won. Instead, we force him to keep hidden deep any thoughts that society deems to be politically incorrect. Thankfully, as trust builds between us, the real Reggie rises steadily to the surface: a warm and witty submariner coming up for air, his vessel crewed by gollywogs and krauts and women who like to do housework whilst their men drink beer and eat steak. In fact, the last email Reggie managed to launch before his laptop battery failed was a great reminder of this forgotten man.

I'd been asking Reggie about his navy life. He sent me two images. One was current: that familiar graphic of the microscopic, spiky red ball from which we are all cowering. The other was from another century, a similarly spiked sphere, only this time huge and grey, chained to the seabed floating twenty feet below the waves. It was a picture of a sea mine, the type hunted and destroyed by Reggie before it had the chance to make contact with larger boats, infect a whole ships company with white-hot, lethal shrapnel. Beneath these two images he explains, points out how similar the two objects appear and that we still can't trust the squareheads. Reggie is joking, of course, doesn't believe for one moment that Germany has engineered the Covid virus, but you try telling his joke down at the student union and see how long you last. You'd be thrown out before you could supp the foam from your Warsteiner for even hinting that a nation which so callously blew your countrymen to smithereens only two generations ago shouldn't be forgiven or above suspicion today.

Yes, I've really enjoyed getting to know Reggie, this despite the fact that the pace of our growing friendship has been slowed by the death of his laptop and the need for him to communicate instead using a marker pen and cardboard signs. Who'd have thought that as I self-isolated I would find myself connecting with a man from a generation I've spent most of my life ignoring. There is a slight downside, though, and it's this: as my affection for Reggie grows so does my sadness at how little I know my own granddad.

Another regular visitor to my lockdown life these days is Mr Bucket Head. Speaking of the little pink devil here he is, sliding past my balcony for the third time in as many days. Unusually this time he stops, hangs outside my window staring at me. I suppose his rope must be snagged, but hey, not my problem if Mrs Wilson has to wait for her chocolate buttons, so I allow my call to Mum and Dad to connect. When it does, unusually Dad is in the picture too, sat close to Mum with his arm around her shoulders. She is nestling back into his and it looks to be a genuine cuddle with not enough space between them to squeeze the dirty secret that they share so I guess that they must be over their tiff. Weirdos, the pair of them if I'm honest, but Mum seems happier than she has done for a while, so my 'wait and see' tactics are vindicated.

I'm not much in the mood for a banal 'what you having for dinner' chat, but there is one new item on my whiteboard that I'd like to weave in to the conversation as I really do need to try and foil the tramp's awful and potentially deadly gameshow plan. Here goes.

'Hey, Mum, did I mention that I found Granddad wandering around in the park? On his own, mind.'

'No, you didn't, love. How is he?'

'How is he? Well, he'd just finished up on the swings and was waiting for his turn on the zipwire so just bloody dandy! How the hell do you think he is, wandering around by himself, but I think you're missing the bleedin' point here!'

'Hey, now think on, Liam! Mind that tone with your mother.'

Oh, so now the big man's all worried about his wife's feelings, is he? Unbelievable! I see my dad through very different, less respectful eyes these days, and his stern rebuke has zero impact. Ignoring him, I continue berating Mum.

'Seriously, you need to speak to someone at the home, Mum, tell them to keep him inside. Shit, he's your fuckin' dad for Christ's sake, and if he was to bump into someone wit—'

'Hey, now that's enough! He's not in prison, Liam. Norman can come and go as he pleases. He's an adult, can do what he wants and I won't tell you again, mind your language.'

I've had enough of his two-faced bullshit. 'Yeah, well, we'd all like to do what we want, wouldn't we? But life isn't like that.'

My parents look puzzled at this rather random, car-bumper-sticker philosophy. I smile thinly, leave them with it and a surly promise to call again in a couple of days.

When I look up from the screen I see that Mr Bucket Head is still there; still hanging, still staring at me. Strange, this, so I go to check out the problem, and that's when I notice that there's something different about him today: a yellow arrow pinned to the rope such that it points down into the bucket. On the arrow is written a single word.

LOOK

I don't understand why, but somehow this simple, cartoon-like arrangement cheers me, my smile broadening further when I look inside the bucket and read the note there.

HEY GRINGO! I KNOW YOU SMOKE, I'VE SMELT IT.
PUT SOME GEAR IN THE BUCKET.
EL CUBETA

El cubeta isn't one of the four Spanish words I know, but a quick google translate tells me that it means 'the bucket', which is a fantastic name for a Mexican drug lord hiding out in north Manchester. I call up using a really dodgy Texan accent.

'*Buenos dias, amigo!* I'm just a simple Christian fella who gits high on the love of my good lord an' shootin' shit. The hash y'all smell belongs to ma buddy 'n' he's mighty clear that I ain't to go touchin' his devil's weed.'

Immediately, the rope yanks Mr Bucket Head back up to the fourth floor, as if in a huff. I wait a while, but there is no reply to my playful refusal to put John's marijuana in the bucket and the levity I was enjoying drains quickly, leaving me feeling deflated and a little stupid. Off to the kitchen to make a coffee.

Standing at the machine I continue to beat myself up for misreading the situation and acting so lame, but this self-recrimination soon froths into anger. She's the one who was basically trying to shake me down for free gear, so why the hell am I feeling like the embarrassed idiot here! When I get back on the balcony I'm still seething a little, simultaneously sipping and grumbling at my hot milky foam when El Cubeta returns, no doubt to double down on his demand for drugs. This time, though, I can see immediately that The Bucket means business and this time I can laugh out loud without fear of appearing foolish.

El Cubeta's normally affable, painted smile has been rubbed out, replaced with a toothy sneer that threatens me from beneath a thin, evil-looking pencil moustache. Eyes that had been wide are reduced to slits, accented with angry eyebrows, but the thing that really cracks me up is the toy gun that's been sellotaped to the handle and is pointing directly at a cuddly toy mounted on the opposite side. The teddy bear has black tape gagging its mouth to prevent it from calling for help. Beneath the gun a cardboard voice bubble tells me that if I don't do as I'm told then the bear gets it. I don't want to risk the accent again or a needless death, so I use my normal voice.

'Okay, okay, you win. I'm getting the gear, just don't shoot the pig or whatever it is.'

It can't have taken me any longer than a minute or so to grab a handful of leaves from John's bedroom cupboard, but I'm too late. When I return the soft toy's head is missing, an open tear spilling out white stuffing where it should have been. I cry out in mock anguish.

'Why, oh, why! When will this senseless killing stop!'

Finally, there is a noise from the balcony above, a happy giggle that's bright and spontaneous and worth the wait.

'Hey, listen, before I put the thing you want in the bucket, I have to ask. Are you a policewoman? Oh, and by the way, you do have to tell me or else you have to cover your eyes and give me a ten-second head start before chasing after me, no peeping either. That's the law.'

Another giggle, this time followed by her voice. 'You raise a good point, but straight back at you. How do I know that you're not a cop? You could have been undercover for years trying to infiltrate El Cubeta's network of balcony buckets distributing chocolate and cocaine to old ladies.'

'Hmmm. Interesting theory, and I'm not saying you're right, but suppose we are both undercover cops then does that mean—'

'Liam Slater! Come on down!'

There have been a few occasions in my life when I have experienced a physical reaction to words (the break-time promise of after-school pain from Tony 'the tooth breaker' Phillips had been one), but this phrase, called across the park in the style of a crazy gameshow host, churns my stomach and weakens my knees. I look towards the taunt and there he is, bawling at me from the middle of the park: the tramp standing with his right arm wrapped around my granddad, his left held high and twisted to his face showing me that he's started his imaginary stopwatch.

'Shit! Listen, I have to go. The weed's in the bucket.'

The race is on.

16

As I run I count. I start at five, to give myself some margin for Mississippi error as well as my initial, dithering delay. Six Mississippi, seven Mississippi, eight and the flat door is open. Another bounding twelve gets me down the fire escape and as I reach the ground I yell a celebratory 'good lads!' for the maintenance crew who've ignored my email and haven't yet installed a security gate to impede me. Three seconds later and that same crew are re-named 'lazy bastards' when a rogue root, bursting through the footpath that they never fix, trips and spins me down into the shrubs they never trim. I don't stop counting, struggle through twenty-four and twenty-five to free myself from the brambles, ignore the thorny stings, use the bush to pull myself back on to my feet and by thirty-five I'm sprinting through the park entrance. I've got twenty-five seconds to cover two hundred metres, to save my granddad from the tramp's tongue. Digging in I leave the gravelly tarmac, feet finding firmer grip, arms pumping and powering me across the open field.

I reach them with four seconds to spare. Hunched over, gagging for air and unable to straighten fully, I claim my prize.

'Right, you've had your fun, arsehole, now give me my granddad.'

'Now, now, Liam, mind your language. It's a family show.'

'Whatever. Just let him go.'

My breathing has found a shallower rhythm and whilst I'm still sucking hard I am able to straighten up and look him in the face, let him know that I mean what I say. Trouble is he is still playing his messed-up game.

'Oooooh, you know, I'd love to let him go, but unfortunately you took sixty-two seconds to get here. Really, so close, and for a while there I thought you were going to make it, but sadly, no… but, a real crowd-pleaser!'

'No! No way! I counted all the way and there's no way it took me more than a minute! No way!'

'Well, my stopwatch says sixty-two so, hey, rules is rules. Did you use one thousand two thousand? I did. It's so much more accurate than that one Mississippi two Mississippi crap.'

I'm not doing this.

'Granddad, come on. I'll take you home.'

I don't think Granddad even tried to move towards me, but if he did then his effort was quickly snuffed out by a tightening arm wrapped around his shoulders. This is getting serious.

'Liam Slater, if you're ready, let's play… Who Wants to Lick an Octogenarian!'

The tramp licks the air close to Granddad's cheek then stares back at me.

'So, what's it going to be, Liam? You gonna gamble? See, as good ol' Norman here didn't get his question right you have a choice to make. Now, let's remind you and the viewers at home of your options. You can either choose a grand for Granddad, go for a double-or-quits question or take one for the team. So, Liam Slater, for a final time I'm asking you, what's it going to be?'

Shit, this is happening! This is actually happening! I'm going to get punched in the face because this time there's no school bathroom window to sneak through, like I did when I left 'the tooth breaker' shouting my name outside the school gates! Think, Liam, think! Just calm down and think about this. I mean, in truth, depending on the subject, of course, what are the chances that a homeless bloke is going to be able to think of a question that you can't answer? You're a final-year student, for Christ's sake, and he's a drop-out! Maybe the double-or-quits question wouldn't be such a gamble after all.

'Look, and I'm not saying that I'm choosing this option, but what's the subject of the double-or-quits question?'

The tramp looks down, puts a finger to his ear and tilts his head as if listening to direction. He is concentrating, nodding and mumbling then snaps back, brightens and looks at me.

'The boys upstairs say that's fine, so I am happy to tell you that, just like your granddad, it's going to be a maths question. Does that help? Come on, Liam, tell everyone what you're thinking, talk us through it.'

You beauty! If I could have picked anything it would be maths! There's no way on this planet that this unwashed scumbag holding my granddad to ransom could possibly think of a maths problem that I can't solve! Worth double-checking, though, see if I can get a clue as to what level of maths we're actually talking about here.

'And you say my granddad got his question wrong. So what was that?'

The tramp squeezes his captive playfully, all the time looking my granddad in the eye whilst he recaps what had happened between them to start the clock that set me racing.

'Well, we had a little chat, didn't we, ol' fella, and then I asked good ol' Norm here, if he had fifteen oranges and three bowls, how many oranges would he put in each one if he split them equally.'

'What, and are you telling me that he got it wrong?'

'Spectacularly wrong, didn't you, Norm, you silly old sod! Got all confused and said that you don't like oranges but you love bananas, didn't you, eh?'

The tramp shakes him gently and Granddad smiles, confused still about who we are but seemingly happy enough to be here. Well, if this example is any indication of what lying Larry Smith thinks is a maths question then it's a no-brainer.

'Double or quits. I'll take the double-or-quits maths question.'

'Good choice, my man, good choice. Right, here goes. And remember, if you get it wrong then you both get licked. So, listen carefully and please, no shouting out from the audience. Okay, to release your granddad, Liam Slater, tell me what number you get if you take the square root of eighty-one and then…'

Nine, it's nine. Square root of eighty-one is definitely nine.

'…then add to that the cube root of one hundred and twenty-five and then…'

Cube root of one twenty-five is five so add that to nine gets me to fourteen. Oh, this really is junior-school stuff, and he thinks he's testing me!

'…then finally add to that the number of brothers that your granddad had and the month of his birthday. Now, Liam, what do you get?'

The number of what? No! You can't do that! That's not maths! Shit, I have no idea, not even able to hazard a guess! Damn it, if this was about Reggie then I could easy answer (two brothers and add six for June), but Granddad! My mind is a shameful blank.

My face must be blank too.

'No? I can see that you're struggling. Tell you what, Liam, you get it right and I'll throw in the trainers.'

Desperate to remember anything, I broaden my focus away from the man himself and try to recall if I've ever heard Mum mention any of her uncles or perhaps talk of birthday get-togethers. I think there's an uncle Bob, lives over near Leeds, but there again that could be on Dad's side? I do know that she always sends me a reminder about Granddad's birthday and I'm pretty sure that that's around March, maybe April?

'Well, look, I shouldn't really do this, but I like you, Liam, so let me help you with the tricky bit. Square root of eighty-one is nine and then if you add to that five then you get fourteen. All you need to do now is the easy, adding-up bit!'

Knobhead. He knows I've got nothing. I could take a guess on March, but as for the brothers, not a clue.

'Brothers and birthday, Liam, brothers and birthday. That's all it is. Surely you must have talked to your granddad about his life at some point when you went to visit him? I mean, I've only known the bloke five minutes and I could tell you the answers. He really is a nice man, you know, Liam.'

Granddad's still smiling, occasionally at me but unable to read the urgency in my eyes that are silently begging him to flash fingers or cough me the answer. More silent moments pass until finally, satisfied that he's won, the tramp ends the game.

'Aw, time's up, I'm afraid. You fancy having a guess anyway? No? Okay, but for the benefit of those playing along at home, the answer was nineteen. Nineteen, Liam. You've got three brothers, haven't you, Norman? Bob, Brian and Roger.'

I knew there was a Bob! Granted, I had him on the other side of the family, but a Bob nevertheless. That leaves the number two to complete the sum, which means granddad was born in February. Of course it's February, not March! March is when I get the annual text from Mum telling me that I've forgotten his birthday, again.

'And he was born on the twenty-seventh of February, Liam, so that makes another five all together to add to the fourteen I gave you earlier.'

Yes, I've done the maths and I've already arrived at the correct answer: that I've completely underestimated you too. I'm not sure what this means, how things will unfold from here. The tramp's rolling his tongue around his mouth now, moistening it! Aw man, I can't let him do this! I need to take the punches, like me and Matt both agreed. After all, that's what the tramp's always wanted out of this, isn't it? He'd told me so, that 'take one for the team' would be his preference. Damn it, I hate pain, but as I psych myself up to demand my right to three smacks in the face the tramp beats me to it, does something that will scar me far worse than a physical attack ever could.

I watch in horror as the tramp slowly removes his arm from my granddad's shoulders, turns him steadily around until they are face to face.

'Liam will take you home now, Norman. It was lovely to meet you.'

They shake hands and the tramp starts to walk away.

'What, so is that it? Are we done?'

The tramp stops but doesn't turn. All I can see is the back of his dirty brown jacket, a perfect mirror for the disgust that I'm feeling at myself as the lesson he's just served me slowly sinks in.

'Oh no, Liam, we are far from done. And after what I've just learned about you, well, it only convinces me that when you do eventually get what's coming to you then, boy, will you deserve it. You really are a self-centred little prick, Liam Slater. See you around.'

17

No sleep for me last night. Too many unresolved and, frankly, disturbing situations charging around inside my head. The tramp's threat had triggered the most nightmarish and riotous scenes: him a huge, bearded monster, slobbering and smashing through trees and walls, obstacles over which I have to scramble as we race to Granddad. And as we run he taunts me, tells me what a cowardly and selfish bastard I am, a perpetual victim happy to blame anything or anyone else because nothing is ever my fault. In the dream he reaches the prize before me but rather than struggle on I simply give up, turn my back, leave the tramp troll towering and dribbling over Granddad.

At this point I'd woken briefly, pricked bolt upright for a moment then slipped back into my dream, only now the scene has changed. I am hidden, out of sight of the tramp and inside Dad's shed. There are others in the darkness with me, faces unseen but all of them known. Smelly's here, sat on one of the lounge chairs, despising me for bullying her. She's holding hands with John, who smiles thinly back at her but fumes as he turns to me, the treacherous best mate who locked him out of his home. Jenny's here too, pissed at my sanctimonious dismissal of her right to do what she feels she must to get through this lockdown in one piece. There is some light, spilling in from beyond a door held open by a woman who looks like something that a ten-year-old Matt might imagine for his ideal girlfriend. Impossibly large breasts, she has, huge red slutty lips too, and they smile as she leans into my face to thank me, but when I ask her for what, the door slams shut and in the total blackness she whispers, 'Thanks for bringing your daddy to me, Liam, for bringing him home from Germany so we can be together.'

It's a cruel dig, the hardest hit of the night.

At this point the dream dissolves into dawn, and I wake, stretch and yawn, recap and salvage from it the materials I'll need to mould a morning reality that I can live with. Whilst I brush my teeth I sculpt, scrub and spit. A final rinse and I'm done, ready to reaffirm my innocence to the man in the mirror.

'See! None of this is my fault! I mean, what the hell chance did I have but to become anything other than me me me?'

Yes, innocent indeed. As innocent as that six-year-old boy who'd sat on a wall minding his own business and yet somehow ended up being blamed for the wreckage of his parents' lives! This vindication of my adult character flaws is all I need to put the nightmares firmly behind me and by the time I settle to sit in the early-morning sunshine, I am once more content and blaming everyone else for everything that's shit. Talking of which there's an awful stench of—

'Hey, gringo! What the hell is that smell? You do realise that when people say they're smoking some good shit it doesn't literally mean they're smoking dog faeces, don't you?'

She's noticed it too then, a cloud of dog-poo stink drifting up and along the balcony from somewhere behind me. The source of the smell is easily found; I can see it from where I sit. It's a squishy shopping bag, lying open on the floor by the wall nearest the fire escape. I don't have to look inside to know that it's filled with dog dirt. God knows what point he's trying to make, but the tramp's done this, leaned across the gap and tossed a bag of dog turds over my wall. Instinctively I hit the switch beneath my table. The ball of fairy lights flashes; the trap still works.

'You can smell it, can't you? It's definitely coming from your balcony.'

Admittedly, I have never seen the girl on the balcony, but somehow I really like her, have found myself thinking about her unexpectedly a couple of times and smiling when I do. So how to tell her that the thing that she can smell is indeed a bag of crap and, yes, it's on my balcony? I could go with the truth, I suppose, but then again, imagine that conversation! No, best to tell a white lie, I reckon. A harmless little story that makes me look good rather than like someone who is being harassed by a homeless bloke because… because, well, and there's the problem: because why is Lying Larry Smith so angry with me exactly? No, it's definitely going to be simpler to fib on this one, get past it and move the conversation quickly along.

'Oh, hello, you! Hey, look, I'm really sorry about the smell but my dog has had an accident. I gave him some apple to try last night and I think it's upset his belly, poor thing. So anyway, how are you finding the lockdo—'

'You have a dog? Wow, I had no idea! I love dogs. What's he called?'

Now I like to pride myself on being a bit of a ninja when it comes to problem-solving but apparently, when it comes to naming imaginary dogs, I'm more your sumo kind of guy and no matter how I grapple with her question my mind remains a big fat blank.

It's already been seconds, a ridiculously long time to simply say the name of your pet dog!

'Are you still there?'

Balcony girl's voice is much louder this time, so loud that it reaches across the road and momentarily halts Reggie as he slides open his door. He looks back over, waves at me as he sits down to eat beans.

'Yep, still here. Me and my dog. You asked what his name is, yeah? Reggie. His name is Reggie.'

'Aw, that is so cute! Hello, Reggie, is your tummy feeling a little poorly this morning?'

Her voice is still raised (in that toddler talk that's so enticing to dogs and old people) and when real Reggie hears his name he looks up from his breakfast, pauses, shrugs and then bends down to pick up one of his answer cards from the floor. When he reappears he's holding a sign high in the air, the one that says 'NO'. Fortunately balcony girl doesn't seem to notice, obsessed as she is with fake Reggie.

'He's very quiet, isn't he? Does he ever bark?'

I'm regretting this now, having to talk about a dog that I don't have and, what's more, one that I'm going to have to get rid of before lockdown finishes! Why the hell didn't I just deny it, say that I had no idea where the smell was coming from! Having said that, at least the lying is becoming easier now, given that all I have to do is describe what I'm looking at.

'Bit sad, really, but no, Reggie can't make a sound. Poor ol' fella had an operation on his throat not long ago. Vet says he might never bark again. Struggles to chew his food too but he does love his baked beans, does our Reggie, don't you, boy? So anyway, I was wondering if I could get your phon—'

'Poor old Reggie can't make a soundy woundy, canny wanny!'

It's as if I'm not here. Balcony girl has given up even feigning interest in anything I might have to say. She's talking directly to my 'dog' now, her gooey words sliding down but also spilling out and over the road to where Reggie is. By this time he's given up on his beans altogether, twisted himself around on his chair so as to better hear the stranger interrupting his breakfast with questions that were initially cute (if not a little over familiar) but now seem to be just an out-and-out piss-take of his unfortunate condition.

'I bet Reggie can wag his tail, though. Can Reggie wag his tail for me?'

A loud knock on my door. Down on the street a white van is parked, engine running. I won't be missed, but I let her know anyway. 'Hey, listen, I think I've got an Amazon delivery. Back in a tick.'

Outside my door there is a parcel, a big one too, abandoned in an otherwise empty corridor at the end of which the lift door is sliding closed. The box isn't heavy so I can easily shuffle it inside with my feet. By the time I've wiped it down and carried it to the balcony to show Reggie, the white van is pulling away from the kerb. Something's happened in my absence because Reggie is standing up now, right at the front of his balcony, and he's waving a sign very enthusiastically, only this time it's the one that says 'YES'.

'Hi I'm back, did you—'

'What's with the old guy? Why is he waving that sign at us, do you think?'

'God knows, never seen him before. Weirdo, eh? Bit of lockdown crazy setting in, probably, but no need to do anything about it, he seems to be okay. But just to be sure, I'll keep an eye on him. So what have you been saying to my Reggie then? He seems very excited.'

Whilst I talk I hold the box up to let real Reggie see it, put my thumbs in the air and motion with my hands for him to calm and sit himself back down.

'Aw, is he? I was just telling him that I'll take him for a walk in the park when all this is over.'

This wasn't exactly how I planned to finally meet the future Mrs Slater, strolling round the park with my imaginary dog and a World War II veteran while all the time getting abused by a tramp who's wearing my shoes, but hey, knowing my luck, the girl on the balcony's probably a size sixteen anyway so what the hell?

'Great, it's a date!'

18

I stayed out on the balcony until quite late last night. Having finally managed to move the conversation on from all things dog (fake Reggie needed his medicine and a rest), me and balcony girl had sat at our respective coffee tables and poured drinks: whisky for me and wine for her. Snacks were shared too, cheesy biscuits brought down by El Cubeta, who, even when I reloaded him with beef jerky, refused to leave until I paid my dues and added another handful of John's precious herb. I reckon we must have spoken between balconies like this for about an hour or so and it felt weird, but in a good way. We skipped all the usual, shallow exchanges that relative strangers typically engage in as they decide whether or not to invest themselves in something more. There was none of that 'where are you from originally' crap, just two friends talking and laughing, as if we had known each other for ages. In fact, so casual was our conversation that, other than her first name, the only things I recall learning about Chloe are that she doesn't trust mushrooms and she doesn't believe in dinosaurs. When she did call it a night, to go back inside and take a bath, there was nothing awkward about our goodbye, no sense that we should swap numbers or arrange to meet again as it was a given that us talking like this was a thing now. If anything, it all felt a bit too pally, really, and as I sat outside, reflected and continued to get pissed, peppered amongst my satisfied grins there were moments of deep concern, doubts that Chloe might be interested in me as anything other than a chatty neighbour.

Because of this nagging flaw in an otherwise excellent start to my quest for a girlfriend, I didn't manage to get to sleep for quite a while after climbing into bed. That's where I should be now, crashed out in my pit and not standing bleary-eyed in the kitchen, waiting for the kettle to boil. It is ridiculously early, especially for a lockdown day! I do remember having a quick look at the stuff I'd got from Amazon on my way to bed so it could be that which has me up and about: a big kid on Christmas Day, impatient to play with his toys.

I collect the box on my way outside, unpack it onto the table and inspect the bow, the arrows, the suckers and pulley. True, these are great things and I can't wait to assemble them into something functional, but apparently, they are not the reason for the churning in my belly because even now that they're laid out on the coffee table, fully inspected and adored, the knot of excitement in my gut remains. If anything it's intensified.

Reggie is up early too, pacing about on his balcony, watching me prepare. I guess it could it be that the buzz I'm feeling is the same as the one that's making him appear so eager for the day to start. Yeah, maybe it's Operation Highwire that has us both psyched: anticipation of reconnecting this isolated veteran back to the world he won and the supplies he—

A sharp breeze whips around the corner and nudges a chair, grinds it against the wall, and even though I see it move from the corner of my eye I still look up, call out just to check that it wasn't her that had made the noise, moving a chair and scraping the floor above me.

'Chloe, is that you?'

No answer, but at least the mystery of why I have butterflies is solved. When the chair moved my first thought should have been, *Damn, I hope the wind drops so I can get the line across*, but it wasn't. My first thought was Chloe. Turns out then that my tingling expectations are – surprise, surprise – far more Liam-centric. I remember that getting the charger across to Reggie is in fact only the first step towards a greater goal because true enough, the charger will bring to life Reggie's laptop and the laptop will reboot Reggie's email, but then the first email that Reggie will see will be from me, asking him to return the favour. Finally, then, I will be able to use Reggie's eyes to see if balcony girl is worth the chase. I don't feel bad about this ulterior motive one bit. It's a win-win, for Christ's sake, so why should I?

As I finish assembling the bits (taking each of the wooden arrows, tying nylon fishing line to one end then attaching a rubber sucker to the other) I reflect on this, eventually having to admit that perhaps this is yet another example of why the tramp loathes me, but again, so what? Bollocks to him too; there's plenty of room in Dad's shed for more of those disapproving glares and I need a fit girlfriend. So, it's with a clear conscience that I stand ready on the balcony, twang the bowstring and lick the plastic red sucker at the end of the first arrow.

'Okay, Reggie, I'm almost ready here. Bit of a breeze swirling, but it comes and goes. I'm thinking that it might be an idea if we both have a say when it's good to go. Can you get something to let me know when it's calm on your end?'

Reggie grabs two pieces of card, then leans on his wall to write on them. When he's done he presents both of them to me, at the same time so there's no chance of a misfire. One card says 'SHOOT', the other 'DON'T SHOOT'. I like his thinking. This is so much clearer than might have been a 'YES' or a 'NO', which could easily mean 'YES' the wind is high or 'NO' it isn't good to send the arrow over. I give him a thumbs-up and explain how I see this working.

'Okay, so when we both agree, I'll send one across. I'll aim for the patio door, so try and keep out of the way, yeah?'

Reggie side-steps, selects and holds a card high. It says 'SHOOT'. I load the arrow into the string and pull my arm back to tension the bow. I really should have tested the power of this thing inside the flat first, but not to worry, I've got four attempts to play with so I can easily calibrate after this first one. The main thing is to not pull the string too hard because if I was to snap it then that would be game over. A gust of wind whips around the corner, so even though Reggie still holds up his 'SHOOT' sign I wait for conditions to improve, and wait, and wait, and now!

At the exact moment that my fingers uncurl from the bowstring Reggie re-evaluates, decides that the wind is too strong and so switches signs. 'DON'T SHOOT', he tells me, but it's too late and the arrow is on its way. I raise my head to watch it go, bang on target as it flies across the road, towing behind it a jet stream of silver fishing line tracing a perfect trajectory and for a moment I doubt Midshipman Mullen's assessment that the launch should have been aborted. Sure enough, though, as the arrow reaches halfway, the breeze he felt pulls the arrow away to the right.

Not only do I miss the patio door but I miss the building, completely.

'Okay, it's okay. No need to panic. Crap shot but first attempt and at least we know now that there's more than enough power in the bow. I'm thinking that I might take the next one a little bit easier actually, for—'

'Liam Slater, what the hell are you up to? A spot of old man-hunting before breakfast? Trying to catch yourself a new granddad? Well, for what it's worth, my advice is to aim for the hip. That's always a weak spot with 'em.'

What the hell is he doing here! Strolling down the road at this time of the morning! Worse than that, why is he speaking to me? I was kind of hoping that we would ignore each other for a while, give this thing between us the time to lose its edge, but there's not much chance of that by the sound of it. Do I answer him, have a dig back? A fairly neutral retort would be the tried and tested 'haven't you got a home to go to?', but I reckon that would feel a tad more abusive than intended, given his situation. Probably best to let him have this one, just ignore him, so I load the second arrow into the bow and call over to Reggie.

'Okay, let's have another go. How's things over there?'

With the bow held at arm's length I drop my chin and sight along the arrow, wait for Reggie to raise his 'SHOOT' sign. He does and its calm at my end too, but this time, rather than fire the arrow on the very second that I get this double green, I take a moment to glance around at the trees near the building, see if there is any wind lurking in their branches, waiting to pounce. There isn't. Everything is still. The only air moving is from my own breathing and its soft hiss helps me focus. It's time, so I draw both breath and bowstring, build the tension steadily until—

'Hurry up, Liam! I've got a bench that needs sitting on!'

The tramp's shout shatters the silence, jolts me and knocks my rock-steady aim. The string slips from the back of the arrow, but only partially, and so the arrow still leaves my hand, flops away and goes tumbling to the street, having travelled less than a car's length from my balcony.

'You stupid prick! I'm here trying to help a veteran out here and all you can do is piss about like the bum you are! And yeah, that's right, knobhead! I said veteran!'

I'm not sure what I expected the outcome to be, but my outburst didn't earn an apology or send Lying Larry skulking on his way. What it does do is get me a very intense stare as the tramp snaps to attention and salutes me, sarcastically.

'Private Knobhead reporting for duty, sir!'

When he drops his salute the tramp uses the same hand to form a fake pistol, points and shoots it in my direction, and so the pattern repeats: a harmless exchange once again twisting into something filled with malice. Point made he then raises his knees sharply in quick succession, stamps his feet as if on the parade ground and turns towards Reggie, salutes him also then stands at ease.

'So where did you serve, fella?'

Despite this being a quite respectful question, Midshipman Mullen is having none of it, has obviously had enough already from a stranger who, let's face it, represents everything that the likes of Reggie despise. Calmly he reaches down towards the table and grabs something leaning against it. In a flowing movement, military muscle memory raises the gun to Reggie's shoulder. The tramp laughs, so Reggie calmly continues, pulls back the hammer and takes aim. Judging from the cracks in his voice, the tramp doesn't think this is so funny anymore.

'Alright, easy there, mate. No offence intended. Look, I'm going to leave you girls to play cowboys and Indians now, and listen, I am genuinely sorry if I offended you, friend, and thank you for your service. I mean that.'

Finally, there is contrition! Admittedly, it has taken the shaky trigger finger of a proud man with little to lose, but it's here nevertheless. Makes me wonder if I've perhaps been overly submissive to the beardy bastard throughout all this, although having said that, my Barry plan didn't work out too well. Still, worth mulling over a change in tactics later, perhaps, but for now I've got a job to do so, as Reggie puts the gun back down and the tramp seats himself on the bench, I load the third arrow.

'Okay, Reggie, let's try and forget about him and get on and do this. Now, I'm going to put plenty behind it this time, so get ready to grab the line if the arrow bounces off the door, yeah.'

Reggie tilts his head slightly and listens for the wind, gives a thumbs-up then raises his 'SHOOT' sign high in front of his face. There's nothing of concern on my side either, so I raise the bow, sight and draw back the arrow until my finger touches my cheek. This is about as much tension as I'd applied to the first arrow but that one had struggled to get through what seemed to me to be a fairly light breeze. Momentum is the key here; the faster an object is flying forward then the harder it will be to deflect from its course, so I crank the bowstring back further until my thumb rubs against my ear. A quick check of the trees and I set the arrow flying and boy does it go, fizzing away from me at a hell of a speed! Fizzing away at a hell of a speed, yes, but the extra power has been at the expense of accuracy.

'Reggie! Look out!'

Now, had I kept my mouth shut then the arrow would have done nothing more than strike his sheet of card, but I didn't: I called out a warning, one that is now speeding past the arrow. My words reach Reggie first. Instinctively he lowers the sign and the arrow clips the top of the card, plants its sucker firmly onto Reggie's forehead.

For a brief moment nothing happens: the arrow stays stuck, Reggie stays standing, wide-eyed and pinned to the spot.

Then the moment passes and all at once, everything falls: the arrow, the sign, Reggie too. As he tumbles he reaches out for the table but manages only to tip it over, dislodging the gun that was leaning against it. A sharp crack rings his balcony like a bell, heralds in a silence so complete, so terrifying that I daren't break it. Reggie will, though, give him a second or two and I'm sure he will, but when he doesn't cry out, panic rises in my throat. Then I remember that the bloke's got throat cancer and is basically a mute! Oh, thank god for that! Cool, now all I have to do is just wait a little longer, give him time to get back on his feet and then I'll shout across, check he's okay, because a fall like that can—

'Oh, Liam, what have you done?'

'Nothing! I've done nothing!'

'Really? Strange, that, because from where I was sitting it looked like you shot an old bloke in the head, which is double strange actually since I specifically remember telling you not to do that very thing. Aim for the hip, I said, not the head. Never the head, Liam, never the head.'

So far the commotion doesn't seem to have brought anyone else out onto their balconies, but if we carry on shouting at each like this then it won't be long and I'd rather that didn't happen until Reggie is standing up again.

I whisper down to the street as loud as I can, 'I was aiming for the door. And keep your voice down, would you!'

Bizarrely, he does. 'Hmmm. I was aiming for the door, Your Honour. Yeah, that'll work, Liam. Case dismissed!'

'What the hell are you going on about? Why would there be a judge? There's nothing wrong with him. He'll be fine.'

'Well, let's find out, shall we?'

With that the tramp strides purposefully across the road, is quickly through the shrub garden and skirting the edge of Reggie's apartment block. When he reaches the base of the fire escape he pauses, glances around to check for onlookers then scampers up the metal stairs. Impressively agile, he is, soon three floors high and level with Reggie's flat. I need to know, so I take the risk of rousing the neighbours and call across.

'Can you see anything?'

The tramp leans as far as he can towards Reggie's flat, peers over the balcony wall then pulls back, shakes his head. My hands start to tremble, the first part of me to consider the possibility that Reggie has been badly hurt. It's been too long and I'm starting to think that I should do more. For example, most people would have already called an ambulance, sent a team of highly trained medics dashing up the stairs bearing stretchers, oxygen bottles and machines that make pinging noises. Not Liam Slater, though, because he knows better and that rather than professional medical care, what Reggie really needs is a dirty old tramp with a pocket full of cigarette dimps staring over the wall at him. Yeah, just what you want when you've fractured a hip!

I grab my phone, hit nine then another nine, but before I type a third the tramp acts, clambers onto the top of the handrail. I wait and watch as Lying Larry grabs the steel frame above his head, swings himself across the gap and plants a perfect dismount on Reggie's balcony. A thumbs-up from me to urge him on, but he doesn't see it, having already dropped out of sight below the wall. As he goes to check on Reggie my finger hovers over the keypad, desperately hoping that I won't need to make the call. A minute or so later and Lying Larry Smith reappears.

'He's fine, Liam, or at least he will be. Looks like the gun went off, but the bullet hit his arm. I've stopped the bleeding, but still, best to get an ambulance.'

'I'm on it.'

As I talk I pace, and only once everything is arranged do I look back over. Unexpectedly, I see that Larry is returning to the balcony through the patio doors! He's been inside Reggie's flat!

'How is Reggie? And where the hell have you been?'

'I've got him comfy enough, stopped the bleeding. How long for the ambulance?'

'They reckon about five or ten minutes. So what were you doing in his flat?'

Larry holds a small box in the air. 'It's something he wants you to have. I told him he's going to be fine, but he insisted I go get it. I think it's his medals. Want me to take a look?'

Although I do get the feeling that this unfortunate incident has changed our relationship for the better, I still don't trust him fully. Whatever it is that Reggie wants me to have I know that I will cherish it, but to someone like Larry, well, it might have monetary value so best not to tempt him.

'No, that's fine. I'd appreciate it if you could bring it over, though. Be nice to have you leave something on my balcony that isn't a bag of shit.'

Larry laughs, makes no attempt at denial. At the top of the street a siren wails and this is the signal for him to leave the scene. I'm not totally happy for Reggie to be abandoned like this, but I don't object as I can fully understand how someone like Larry wouldn't want to be found stood over a gunshot victim. Anyway, the medics are almost here and it won't be long before Reggie will be getting the care he needs, so yeah, everything's worked out just fine. Still, it's a bit of a bummer that I'll have to wait a while longer to find out what Chloe looks like, but that's okay.

Time for a well-deserved breakfast, I reckon.

19

On balance I think it's best that I stay inside for a bit, give the ambulance crew time to load Reggie and be on their way. Not that I don't care, of course I do, but what would be the point of me just hanging about, watching them do their thing? It's not like I'd be helping, and just suppose one of the medics was to glance up, ask if I saw what had happened. That would be me, slap-bang in the middle of something that, when all said and done, was just an accident. Okay, so I fired an arrow, big deal. Reggie knew all about what was going on and it was his decision to hide his face instead of keeping an eye out. True, my arrow did hit him, but from what Larry said, it was Reggie's own gun that did the real damage. In fact, when you think about it, I'm no more to blame than Larry because if he hadn't been winding Reggie up then Reggie wouldn't have pulled back the hammer to threaten him and ultimately it was that single act which ensured that the bullet would be fired when the gun hit the ground and shoot Reggie in the arm. Being inside for a while also gives me a good excuse to have a full English, which is something I've been trying to avoid in order to keep those Covid curves at bay. I love a fry-up, though, and when all's said and done, I am but a man.

Ten minutes later, as the sausages finally brown and the bacon starts to spit, I do feel a smidgen of guilt, but it isn't nearly enough to stop me from stacking a fried egg and sliced pig high between thick slices of toasted bread. Five scoffing minutes after that, having vowed that this shall be the last digression until I've been on my date with Chloe, I wipe brown sauce and yellow yolk from my plate and chin, and return to the balcony.

The scene that greets me is not the one that I was expecting.

For starters, the ambulance is still here; rear doors open, but as far as I can tell, unattended. In front of the ambulance there is a police car, parked at a weird angle to the kerb with its lights flashing silent blue and guarded by a single, uniformed officer. There's a second car abandoned closer to the park, a silver something-or-other but not a vehicle I recognise.

'What you reckon, Liam? Covid? Yeah, I reckon Covid got him.'

I haven't fully processed what's going on yet, so Matt's question doesn't register and can't be answered properly.

'What? What you talking about, Matt?'

'Your mate, the old bloke who's been grooming you. Must be Covid, eh? Otherwise, why all this malarkey?'

I must admit, this does seem to be an awful lot of fuss, people and time just to get Reggie and his injured arm down off his balcony and on his way to the hospital. Maybe the fall did more damage than Larry had been able to find in the short time that he'd spent with him. A fractured hip, perhaps?

'Oh, and congrats on the trainers too. You and the tramp kissed and made up?'

Turning to where Matt is pointing I recognise immediately what I'm looking at and dash towards them: my beloved trainers set neatly on the table. Each shoe in turn is inspected, checked for damage, and as I cradle them I can hear myself talking, telling them how they've been missed and how I'll never let them out of my sight again, and even though I know I'm setting myself up to be mocked, I don't care that Matt can hear me. I mean every word and I especially mean the nod of appreciation as I wave to Larry, who is sat on his bench watching the reunion that he's orchestrated. Larry nods back and our relationship takes another step in the right direction.

'What's in the box?'

Matt's spotted something else. Having only had eyes for the sexy and perfectly formed pieces of leather and lace that I'm still caressing, I hadn't noticed the small wooden box sat next to them, but now I remember. Larry had shown me something when he had been on Reggie's balcony, a box that Reggie had asked him to give to me. This must be it.

On top of the box there is a note:

Please always wear the gloves when handling.

Reggie must really care about whatever it is that's kept safe by this worn and well-loved oak case. The box has a single, brightly polished brass hinge and opposite that there's a small brass clasp. I open the clasp and lift the lid. Inside there is a pair of white gloves, neatly folded, and when I take these out the treasure that Reggie has given me is revealed. I am humbled instantly.

'It's his medals, Matt. Reggie's medals from when he was in the navy.'

'Cool. How many? Could be worth a few quid. Hey, maybe you could sell 'em and take your trainers out for a nice romantic meal.'

Ignoring him, I pull the gloves on. They are by no means clean, well-used and full of dark smudges, and being made for hands much smaller than mine, the gloves barely reach my wrist. Still, they will serve their purpose, keep the oils on my fingers from tarnishing the metal that Reggie wants so badly to protect, but before I have lifted the first medal from the box, Matt interrupts.

'Hey, Liam, something's happening. I think they're bringing him out.'

Across the road the door of the apartment block opens. A woman dressed head to toe in dark green steps outside and holds the door open for the rest of her crew who are also dressed in green but wearing jackets that are sectioned with double-striped high-vis yellow bands. Between these two medics there is an orange stretcher and on the stretcher is Reggie, secure beneath a white cover held in place by thick black straps. It looks to me as though the same mischievous wind that slapped the arrow onto Reggie's head hasn't quite finished messing with the old fella yet, so I call down.

'Hey, mate, now I'm not telling you how to do your job, but it looks like the wind has blown the cover over your patient's face. Might make it difficult for him to breathe, yeah?'

By this time the medics are at the rear of the ambulance. Only one can be seen from where I am; the other has climbed inside to help load Reggie into the vehicle. The man outside finishes lowering the concertina support frame of the stretcher to the ground, secures it in place then turns to me.

'Couple of things, pal. For one, telling me how to do my job is exactly what you are doing. Having said that, for two I must also say good catch. I'll move it.'

The medic leans over, stretches across Reggie to grab the offending sheet but stops halfway then straightens back up.

'Oh yeah, I remember now! He is struggling to breathe but that's because – oh, what's the correct medical term… oh yeah, that's it, because he's dead. Now admittedly, it's been a while since I was at medical school, but I do remember something about death being a problem when you're trying to breathe. But hey, you're the expert, so what d'you reckon? Should I uncover his cold, lifeless face and see how that goes or maybe just crack on and get him to the morgue?'

'What you talking about, dead? He can't be. See that bloke over there on the bench? He was talking to him less than twenty minutes ago and he was fine then.'

We both look towards to the bench I'm pointing at and we both see that it's empty. Weird, that, because only moments ago Larry had been sat there, watching intently and taking a close interest in everything that was going on. There's no point in me trying to explain this to the medic, though, because he's already made his mind up about me, and as he walks around the ambulance to climb into the driver's seat, he pauses to take a final pop.

'Oh, and I'm not telling you how to do your job, pal, but mime artists are usually a lot, lot quieter.'

Mime artist? What the hell is he going on about? I look to Matt for support but get none. He is grinning at me, enjoying the joke at my expense that I don't quite get yet.

'He does have a point, Liam. I mean, look at what you're wearing! A tight black crew neck and a pair of white gloves. Jesus, you look like you're going to a Marcel Marceau convention or summat. Shit, imagine that, a room full of 'em. You'd think you'd gone deaf, wouldn't you?'

'You do realise that mime artists can actually talk, don't you? I mean, they'd probably all be chatting about how to look like you're trapped in a box or can't find the door in a wall or something. They're not actually mute, you know.'

Matt thinks about this for far too long.

'Well, you say that, but have you ever actually heard one?'

Unbelievable, and I'm about to tell him what an idiot he is, but as I turn towards him I catch a glimpse of my reflection in the patio doors. The accuracy of his description shocks me into silence and my mime is complete. I can't get the gloves off fast enough, squash them back into the box, checking as I do to be sure that Larry didn't see me make a fool of myself because the last thing I need is to give him ammunition that could threaten what I think might be the start of a fragile truce. Thankfully the bench is empty still.

'So do you think he was just winding me up then? The ambulance bloke, I mean. About Reggie being dead?'

'Could have been, I suppose, but I don't think that them type of people are into making jokes about dead geezers. Nah, something's definitely not right. I mean, why all the coppers for a start?'

Matt's spot on. Not only are there still policemen guarding the building entrance but, on the balcony, I can see two others milling around, both of them wrapped in those white disposable overalls that you see in TV show crime scenes. In those same shows there is often an innocent man, wrongly accused and then ran out of town just before the truth emerges, always too late for him to rebuild his shattered life. Somehow, I feel like I'm that man; a dark foreboding is tickling my guts and giving me a compelling urge to disappear back inside the flat. I'm about to do so when Chloe shouts down.

'Hey, Liam, what's going on? And how's Reggie today?'

Before I can answer her Matt jumps in, over-eager to pay a grisly homage to his favourite Tarantino movie. 'Reggie's dead, babe, Reggie's dead.'

'Oh no! You must feel awful, Liam! How did that happen?'

On hearing about the death of fake Reggie, a dog who she felt she had bonded with and would one day take a for a walk, Chloe loses interest in the scene unfolding on the opposite balcony. I know I have to address her upset but I also know that I have to choose my words cleverly here so that Matt doesn't pick up on anything that he feels might need clarifying. If he does, if he questions who Reggie the fake dog is, then that will surely blow my cover and any chance of ever hooking up with Chloe.

'Well, he was old, as you know, and he had been ill for a while, so not totally unexpected. But still, it is very sad.'

It actually is too and only when I hear myself telling her this does the reality of what is happening here start to sink in. Reggie might really be dead and for the rest of my lockdown I will have to look out onto an empty balcony where once stood someone who was slowly becoming a friend.

'Oh dear, well, I am so sorry to hear that, but like you say he was old and from what you were telling me the other day, incontinent too. It can't have been pleasant for him, that, messing on the balcony, and at least you won't have to collect his poo anymore, eh, Liam?'

It's a rhetorical question, not that I could have answered it convincingly anyway and certainly not well enough to wipe the disgust from Matt's face.

'Did I hear that right? You collected his poo?'

Matt knows that this simply can't be true but rather ridiculously he stares at me hard, demanding an actual denial. This is something I can't give him. She'll hear me and I simply can't risk losing Chloe's sympathy or trust. Damn it, now I wish I really was a mime artist, able to slide hands smoothly through the air, pop knees and elbows and twist my face to tell Matt silently that 'no, idiot, I do not pick up old men's turds, but I did create a fake dog, sadly now dead and that did poo a lot, but I only did this so that I could have a shot at banging the girl from the balcony above even though I'm still not sure she's worth the effort because the real Reggie, sadly now dead, never told me if she's a heifer or not'.

In my desperation I actually begin to try to mime this

but lose Matt completely, having only managed to show him that I think he's an idiot. Time for more ambiguous words.

'Yep, no more picking up Reggie's poo for me, I guess, Chloe.'

There's a rarely seen expression, one that combines utter disgust with abject disbelief, and that's what Matt's face is doing now: widening his lips into a silent scream and bulging his eyes, begging me to tell him that I'm joking. I can't, though, and when the moment of opportunity to do so has passed, stretched into something awkward between us, he leaves the balcony and me with no doubt how he feels about this revelation.

'Jesus, Liam, you sick bastard. I don't even know who you are anymore.'

I think I'll leave too now, go and spend some time alone with Reggie's medals. I make my excuses to Chloe, arrange to be outside later on for a drink in memory of fake Reggie and then return inside. It's as I'm sliding the door closed that I see something down on the street that rekindles the same feeling of unease that I'd had earlier, when I'd first noticed the scene of crime officer rooting around on Reggie's balcony.

Larry is back, but he's not back on his bench. He is standing across the road, near to the silver car that I don't recognise. He is talking to a tall, thin man who is wearing a dark grey suit and the man in the dark grey suit is writing things into his notebook. Something is going on down there, something bad, but worrying about that will have to wait. For now I need to get back inside, give myself some quiet time to say goodbye to Reggie.

20

As it turns out, grieving for Reggie is one of the hardest things I've ever had to do. I don't mean hard in a hard-hitting, emotional sledgehammer type of way, though, no. I mean hard as in extremely difficult.

Ten minutes I've been on the couch. Ten dry-eyed minutes since I took Reggie's medals from the box, laid them out on the coffee table and began what I thought would be a pretty straight-forward grieving process. So why aren't I sobbing or sighing or sniffing as I inspect these pieces of metal which, apart from his knackered laptop, I'm thinking are just about the only evidence left to show that Reggie was ever here? And then I remember.

This is Helen bloody Mirren all over again.

Back in sixth form Helen Mirren had been one of the first women to be given a place on my guilty-pleasures list. For well over three years that platinum-blonde pensioner had held a top-three spot, usually jostling for pole position with Dawn French and that Bond girl who used to be a bloke. Whenever I watched Helen, I would always reaffirm two things: yes, I definitely would, and yes, I definitely would tell my mates. Until last year, that is, when me and John popped round to his dad's house to watch the *Fast and Furious* spin-off *Hobbs & Shaw* that she starred in.

Like his son, Mr Kelly is a bit of a flash git, particularly when it comes to tech, and I'm in no doubt that this unexpected invite had only been texted so that he could brag about his brand-new, ultrathin, 4K 'look at me bitches' sixty-five-inch UHD TV. Regardless of his motive, though, I had to admit, that shiny smooth monolith of technology was a breath-taking bit of kit. Of course, just like every other household in the country that makes the mistake of allowing a man to buy the TV, it was far too big for the room, but hey, that was no fault of that magnificent screen. I loved it utterly and when it was brought to life and doing its thing the crispness of the picture really did take your breath away, made you feel as though you could just reach in from the sofa and grab the steering wheel or punch the villain.

Then Helen had walked into the room and everything changed.

Clad in black leather, she'd been, and initially sassy, but it had taken only one horrifying, high-definition close-up for that mass of treacherous pixels to reveal the truth. Sags, bags and blemishes were left with nowhere to hide. I felt dirty for ever having fancied her, the graceful beauty which I'd admired for so long exposed as nothing more than an illusion, something which only existed when watched on a laptop or phone.

So with that, Mirren was not only out of my top three but off the list for good, and remembering that day now helps me understand why it is that I'm sat here on my couch wondering how much Reggie's medals might be worth rather than mourning his passing.

And the reason I'm not weeping is this: grief, it turns out, is the high-definition TV of emotions, and the clarity of it does not allow you to blur the truth.

Anger, excitement, happiness, all that stuff can be easily feigned or exaggerated by those feeling them, often so convincingly that for a short while at least you start to believe you really are pissed at your mate for being late or genuinely do like Mum's crappy gift. But when it comes to grief? Not a chance! You simply can't kid yourself or invent a memory you know to be a lie and then turn it into something real enough to make you feel a genuine sense of loss. So, I can't pretend to miss Reggie any more than I could've pretended that Mirren still did it for me when I saw her on that huge, brutally honest screen, and just as John's dad's UHD TV had lifted the veil on Helen Mirage, so my lack of grief for Reggie cannot be denied. It simply is what it is and the thing that's gone is what it was: a fun little project to occupy my lockdown days. Sitting here beating myself up for being unable to mourn a bloke who used to stand on the opposite balcony is not going to change that.

What I am starting to feel, though, is a little bit bored. Time to go and put the kettle on, I reckon. It's been a while since I've talked to Mum too, so I need to do that after lunch then grab a snooze before getting ready for my balcony blind date with Chloe. Strange how I do this when I know we're going to talk – get showered and ready, that is – but doing so definitely puts me in a better frame of mind and makes me lift my game for what is, after all, effectively a date. I just wish I knew what she looked like and with Reggie gone that's not going to be—

Three loud bangs.

I have a pretty good idea who is outside my door. It's the man in the dark grey suit. I can't be sure how long his authoritative rap has me frozen to the spot, but my response is delayed sufficiently to earn me a second volley of knocks, this time punctuated with my name.

'Mr Slater. Mr Liam Slater.'

Shit, this is precisely what had put me on edge when I saw Larry talking to him, the inevitable calling copper, and I immediately regret wasting the last quarter of an hour on Reggie and his medals instead of getting my story straight. A bigger problem than what I will say, though, is what Larry has already told him. The pair of them were definitely talking and if what I say doesn't match up then that's—

Three more bangs and time's up. Coming, ready or not, and I have no choice but to open the door. The man behind it is a lot more impressive than when I had seen him from the balcony, a lot taller and broader, and the eyes above his mask are very intimidating.

'Detective Sergeant Miller. Mind if I come in for a chat?'

This is a rhetorical question; he's already inside.

'Sure. What's this about?'

'You took your time answering the door, Mr Slater.'

It's a random thing to say, but Miller's question tells me without doubt that he suspects or perhaps even knows something. Damn it, Larry, what the hell have you told him? As uncomfortable as the insinuation is, though, it does force me to accept that playing dumb with him is going to be a far too high-risk strategy. Too much detail won't be a good idea either; I'd be bound to give him more than he's got already from that treacherous tramp. Yeah, my best and probably only option is to let him take the lead, answer his questions but with as little of the truth as necessary.

'I was just in the bathroom. Sorry, but what is this about again?'

Apart from that initial glare when I had first opened the door, Miller hasn't looked at me since he entered. His eyes have been too busy scanning the flat and he continues to do this as he answers my question.

'Reginald Mullen. It's about Reginald Mullen.' Now the detective does look at me. 'Do you know a Mr Reginald Mullen, Mr Slater?'

Here we go. Remember, tell the truth but don't embellish. Answer his questions but don't elaborate.

'Yes.'

I think this is a good start, but I get the feeling that Miller doesn't agree.

'Yes what? You knew him as a friend, a neighbour, a what exactly?'

As he digs he moves towards the balcony but stops at the coffee table, looks down with interest at Reggie's medals box.

'Well, we've never actually met, so difficult to say. You see, I didn't know him at all before all this lockdown stuff started. It was only once that had happened that we just swapped a few emails and waved across to each other in the morning, that's all.'

As soon as I finish talking, I know that I've said too much. Neighbour would have been fine, should have just said neighbour.

'Emails, you say? And why would a young lad like you be emailing an old age pensioner, Mr Slater?'

And so it begins. Can't mention emails without mentioning my offer to help. Can't mention help without mentioning his failing laptop battery. Can't mention his laptop without mentioning Operation Highwire and can't mention that without explaining how I came to fire an arrow that hit Reggie on the head and set in motion a chain of events that would ultimately lead to his death. So, with my cunning strategy in tatters after only one simple exchange I spill all, tell Miller how me and Reggie had agreed a plan, bought the things I'd need to get John's battery across to him and how the third arrow had struck and felled Reggie, discharged his gun and put a bullet in his arm, an injury from which he would sadly die less than fifteen minutes later. There, it's all out, and yes, I'm kind of involved, but it's the truth and blatantly an accident, and so other than the formality of a visit to the cop shop to make a statement, it's over. I feel a huge relief.

'Well, that all makes perfect sense, Mr Slater. Just a couple of things to wrap this up, if you don't mind, and then I'll be on my way. These medals, for instance, I'm assuming that you weren't awarded them.'

Why do I get the feeling that this isn't just a wrap-up? Far too much Columbo in his attitude for me, that old 'lull the suspect into a false sense of security' routine. Is that what I am here, a suspect? But of what? I've already told Miller everything about what happened.

'Oh no, course not. They were Reggie's but he gave them to me.'

And here we go again. Can't mention the medals without mentioning a dying man's wish for me to have them. Can't mention Reggie's dying wish without mentioning the tramp hearing it and can't mention the tramp without—

'His dying wish, you say?'

'Yes. Whilst I phoned an ambulance this tramp – Larry, I call him, but don't know his real name – well, he clambered up the fire escape to check out how Reggie was, and whilst he was there Reggie asked him to fetch his medals from the flat and give them to me.'

Miller doesn't react to this new information, at least not that I can see. He's turned his back on me, slid open the balcony door and stepped outside. I feel compelled to join him there and as he stares across at Reggie's balcony he asks another, rather random question.

'So, you ordered the bow and arrows online, you say. I guess you have proof of that then, the date and such?'

'Yes, yes. You want to see the order confirmation? I can get the—'

'No, that won't be necessary for now, Mr Slater, just don't delete anything, if you wouldn't mind, including the emails you swapped with Mr Mullen. Now, if I remember correctly, you say you fired three arrows in total. The first two missed and the unfortunate third struck the victim. That correct?'

Victim! That's a hell of a strange choice, isn't it? The deceased, Mr Mullen, the crinkly old dead dude; all of these would have sat easier with me, but the copper said victim!

'Erm, yes, that's right. The third shot was—'

'And how many arrows did you buy again, Mr Slater?'

'Four. It was a set. A bow and four arrows, but—'

'And are those the arrows that you bought?'

Why is he looking behind me when he asks this? He should be pointing around, at the building opposite to start with then somewhere to the right of it, past the fire escape and finally down at the shrubbery outside my block. That's where the arrows fell, I told him this, so why the hell is he nodding his head firmly towards the floor directly behind me?

'Those. Leaning against the wall. Are they the arrows you bought?'

I feel confused and slightly sickened by his insistence, and I don't want to look around at where he is now pointing, but I do. There, stacked against the wall in a messy bundle of fishing line, are four arrows. My four arrows, three of which I had fired across the road but that are now back where they started. Open-mouthed but unable to speak words, I look up at Miller. I wish he looked confused too, but he doesn't. His face is rock-solid in its conviction that everything I've just told him is a lie.

'Okay, Mr Slater, I'm going to need you to help me understand this a little more. Probably better if—'

'Are you arresting me?'

'No, I'm simply—'

'Well, get out then, please. I've told you everything I know, so please could you leave now?'

A silent standoff ensues. There's Miller, standing firm and mulling over his options, no doubt recalling guilty men who've slipped from his grasp, walked free from court behind smart-arsed lawyers armed with thick brown files loaded with technicalities, wondering how far he can push this with no witness and no warrant, and opposite him there's me, fidgeting and desperately trying to remember episodes of *NCIS*, wondering if fictional Miami law holds sway in Manchester.

Apparently, it does.

Miller looks pissed off as he brushes past me and walks silently back through the lounge. At the door he twists the handle and pulls it open, but before stepping out into the corridor he turns and speaks in clear, instructive tones that leave me in no doubt about his intention to get back here as quickly as a judge permits with both a warrant and a constable.

'See you soon, Mr Slater – oh, and please, I know I don't need to tell you this, but I'd rather if you didn't go anywhere for the next couple of hours. Also if you wouldn't mind, try and leave things as they are in your flat, in particular those medals, the arrows and that pair of very expensive-looking trainers. Any questions before we meet again?'

I do actually. 'Have you spoken to anyone else in the building? Chloe in the flat above?'

'I have. She a friend of yours?'

'Kind of. We talk from our balconies, but we've never actually met. Which is why I was wondering if you could tell me what she looks like, you know, her body type, for example.'

Miller shakes his head and walks out of the flat.

In for a penny and all that, so in desperation I shout

down the corridor after him, 'Aw, come on! I answered all your questions! Gymnast, runner, wrestler, swimmer or slob? Just pick one!'

He's in the lift, already pressing buttons and the doors are sliding shut, but before they close completely, Miller shouts back, 'Swimmer.'

Result!

21

My satisfaction at being able to click in place a third piece of the Chloe jigsaw (her sweet, sexy voice and razor-sharp wit can now be laid next to a toned and shapely body) is short-lived. As soon as the door closes, alone in the flat again, I'm forced to consider the last few minutes spent with Miller and his apparent rejection of my version of events. And add to that his barely veiled threat that I mustn't touch anything, that I'm not to tidy away Reggie's medals or move my trainers? Why the hell should that be a thing? I mean, it's not as if he had to coax any facts from me; I told him openly about the medals, that they'd belonged to Reggie, and up until his parting comment, we hadn't even mentioned shoes. Weird, but none of it nearly as puzzling as those bloody arrows, sat out there on the balcony and I know that these got a mention on his 'do not touch' list, but sod it, I have to go and pick at least one of them up, check for certain that it is indeed one of those that I fired across the road.

Back on the balcony I hunch down before them, consider them as a group of four for a moment and then finally select one to inspect closer. I pick it up, hold it in the light above the shadow of the balcony wall and recognise immediately the soft red sucker tips that I had stuck on one end. The long trail of fishing line, fixed with Sellotape to the other, is unmistakeably mine too. I can feel the furrows in my brow deepening with the mystery. This just doesn't make any sense! How the hell can—

'How came'st thou in this pickle?'

Shock bolts me upright, throws the arrow from my hands, and I almost tumble over the wall as I grasp at it to prevent it falling back into the shrubs for a second time. Only when the arrow and my composure are gathered do I turn towards the voice, to the tramp stood smiling on the fire escape.

'What's that supposed to mean?!'

'Not familiar with Shakespeare, Liam? It's from *The Tempest*. In layman's terms it basically means you're fucked, mate.'

'What the hell did you say to him! And don't deny it, I saw you talking to Miller in the street before he came to see me!'

The tramp looks sternly at me and points at the arrow. 'Talking of Miller, I thought he said that you weren't to touch anything. Could be seen as tampering with evidence if you were to drop that into the street, for example. Best put it back where you found it and don't—'

'Hang on a minute, how do you know what Miller said? Have you been here all the time?!'

Of course he has, and as this realisation sinks in I simultaneously solve the mystery of the homing arrows.

'Shit, you put the arrows back here, didn't you! Why on earth would you do that?!'

'Ah, so many questions, Liam. Look, why don't you grab a seat and calm down and I'll explain what's going on, eh?'

I do need to sit: the weight of his as yet unknown but ominously dreadful purpose is sapping the strength from my legs. The tramp makes himself comfortable, perches on the fire-escape railings and waits for me to sit.

'Comfy, Liam? Good, then I'll begin. Now as to your first question, you're correct. I did talk to Miller, but you're wrong to think that I was telling tales on you. No, I didn't even mention you to be honest, spent most of my time asking if he had a gun, if I could see his badge, if he knew Inspector Morse, you know, stupid shit like that. So, you can relax because I—'

'Bollocks! I'm not buying it. You expect me to believe that all the time you were with him you only asked divvy questions like some big, hairy eight-year-old kid?'

The tramp looks pleased. 'Exactly! And listen, hold on to that thought, Liam, because you're going to need it. Now, as for whether or not I've been here all the time, I'm surprised you have to ask! You know me well enough by now – I wouldn't miss a moment of watching your sad little ass squirm – but more than that, I needed to know if Miller was good at his job or not, which, by the way, he definitely is. Yeah, he hit all the right spots, Liam, couldn't have asked for more.'

'What are you going on about, hit all the right spots?'

'Clues, Liam, clues. Miller got them all, at least all the ones I need him to have. The medals, the trainers and, oh, let's not forget them pesky arrows which, as you quite rightly pointed out, I managed to put back when he was on his way up to see you. Jesus, that was a close call, though, I can tell you. That dopey twat of a neighbour of yours was out, thought he'd never leave, but he did, just in time too. Lucky that, 'cos otherwise my plan wouldn't work.'

I really have no idea where he is going with all this. Did he say plan? These are the ramblings of a crazy man, a deranged nutter that thinks he's some kind of master criminal who's just pulled off the perfect crime, this even though he knows damn well that I've already told Miller the truth about what happened! At least I think I told him everything about Operation Highwire. Didn't I? I scan search our conversation to find the relevant bits, check they're good, but as my mind reviews so the tramp seemingly reads it.

'See, I'm thinking that you probably do have emails and stuff to back up any story you've got about firing arrows across at Reggie. But if those arrows are still on your balcony then that ain't worth shit 'cos as far as Miller's concerned you never fired 'em! Think that might be a bit of a problem for you, Liam?'

My face is a blank and the tramp leans towards it, shaking his head sympathetically.

'No? Still not getting it? Well, look, we don't have much time because I reckon that it's going to take Miller less than an hour to get the warrant he needs, and while he does that, you, my friend, are going to be very busy getting the thing that you'll need to save your scrawny neck. So, listen, and listen good. First, you need to know is this. When I clambered on Reggie's balcony to see how he was – well, I tell you, it was a bloodbath, mate. Head burst right open, it was, barely anything left of his face, and I got to be honest with you, I crapped myself. I mean, there I was, an undesirable homeless guy clomping about all over his balcony, leaving my footprints in a dead bloke's brains, and that's when it struck me, Liam. These aren't actually my shoes! So once I realised this then—'

'Wooaahh. Just back this up! He wasn't dead, you spoke to him! You told me you spoke to Reggie!'

The tramps face lights up. 'I know! Brilliant or what! Spur of the moment, that, bought me the time I needed to have a good ol' think about how to screw you over proper. See, I already had you on the balcony, Liam, the shoes did that, but I do know how them coppers love banging on about motive and shit, and that's when it hit me. Burglary! So, I dodged inside Reggie's flat while you were on the phone, thought about grabbing his shitty laptop, but when I picked it up, that's when I saw them. Reggie's medals. Sweet or what! Just the sort of sentimental crap I knew you'd go for, and man, the minute I saw your little face when I shouted over that Reggie wanted you to have 'em, I knew I was golden.'

I open my mouth to speak, to interrupt him, and to be fair he waits for me to make a noise, but we both know I have nothing to say; we both understand that my silent gape is only a floundering attempt to stem the flow of what is starting to build into a very convincing and frankly worrying scenario. He's waits a moment longer, laughs with delight then ploughs on.

'So, to recap, Liam. Miller's got you at the crime scene with a motive. All I need now is to put the gun in your hands, which is impossible, right? Got to admit, I thought so too, but turns out we're both wrong, and trust me, even though this is really bad news for you, I think you'll appreciate the beautiful simplicity of it. See, I was just about to wipe the gun down – no fingerprints better than just Reggie's, right? – but when I went to grab a tissue from my pocket, I dropped the box, and hey ho, along with the medals, a pair of white gloves fell out!'

He pauses, closes his eyes and holds his bearded chin as though deep in thought. When he eventually speaks again it's in a purposeful whisper that forces me to concentrate hard on what he says.

'Please always wear the gloves when handling. Recognise them words, do you, Liam?'

I do. These were the exact instructions that had been printed neatly on the card that the tramp had given me along with Reggie's bequeathal. Word for word they are, and the only way that this arsehole could have recalled them so flawlessly is if he had written that note.

'You know, I wasn't sure if you'd actually fall for that one, Liam, actually use the gloves, 'cos you're such a rebel, but when I saw you wearing 'em, having that barny with the ambulance bloke, well, I tell you, it was all I could do to stop meself from running over, screaming out "gotcha" and doing a little victory dance!'

Why he's so pleased with himself about this particular detail I have no idea. The tramp's over-confidence is ironically reassuring, though, allows me to find my voice, because when you actually break it all down, his little scheme is about as convincing as a Facebook tax return.

'So what if I did! Like I told you, Miller knows all about the medals, so why the hell is he going to bothered if I nicked a pair of old gloves or not?'

'Hmmm. Damn it, I think you could be right, Liam. How did I miss that! Why indeed would a copper be interested in a pair of old gloves that you'd used to look at the medals that you may or may not have nicked? Guess I'm getting a bit carried away but... hey, hang on a minute! What if those old gloves were smudged with gun oil from a murder weapon, eh? You reckon Miller might be interested in 'em then?'

'You didn't... tell me you didn't, you bloody maniac!'

'Wish I could, pal, wish I could. But I can't, 'cos I did, and now Miller's got everything he needs to put you behind bars for a long time, Liam. Murder scene shoes, gun gloves sat with the victim's medals and alibi arrows you never fired.'

Lying Larry Smith leaves these words hanging, looks away, across towards Reggie's balcony as if to give me privacy whilst I mull this over. The first thing I mull, though, isn't his what I realise now to be a fiendishly clever scheme but the nickname I gave this twat days ago, back when my future did indeed promise bars but of the city variety, bright blingy bars where I'd celebrate yet another deal closed, drink afternoon cocktails with sharp-suited colleagues and get mobbed by very fit girls. Yes, he is no longer a liar, this man; Larry Smith is a teller of truths that, to be honest, any jury in the country might well believe. My second mull, therefore, is that I am indeed in serious shit here and I feel sick.

'So, here's the deal, Liam. You give me ten grand and I make all this go away. I go to Miller, tell him everything about what I've done, back up your version of events to the very last detail. How's that sound?'

'I'll tell you how it sounds, it sounds like bullshit, you fuckin' freak! Do you really think I'd trust you to do that? To admit you lied, nicked stuff from a dead bloke, not to mention obstruction of justice or whatever they call it when someone screws the coppers over. So no, thank you, stick your deal up your arse. I'd rather take my chances with a judge!'

I'm not trying to call his bluff here; I genuinely believe this. The man simply can't be trusted and I can't help thinking too that even if I was to take a chance, enter some kind of deal and put a down payment on his services then he's just as likely to twist that too, take this new evidence to the coppers, tell them that he'd seen everything and that I'd tried to shut him up with hush money. No, this stops now.

And perhaps it would have done had it not been for what came next.

'Remember me saying that I didn't tell anything about you to Miller when I was with him in the street, you know, being all simpleton and that? See, I'm thinking okay, I probably will get in a right load of shit if I suddenly blurt out the truth, but then again, really, how hard are they gonna come down on a homeless guy with learning difficulties, eh? I mean, even if I did get given time, what we talking? Six months max in some cushy little open prison over Christmas? Not too shabby that, I can tell you, and I gotta admit, before you came along, I was leaning towards headbutting some random dude at the bus stop around late October anyway.'

The tramp slides down from the handrail and stands, faces me, arms open. 'So what you reckon now, Liam? This little scheme of mine's a win-win, yeah! The bloke at the bus stop gets to hug his grandkids without bleedin' all over 'em, I get a nice turkey dinner and you get to put all this shit behind you once and for all.'

Actually, this all makes some kind of messed-up sense, but he seems to have forgotten that there is, in fact, one loser here: the bloke who needs to hand over ten grand from his savings pot. Shit, it's hard enough asking Dad for a couple of hundred for rent (hence my perpetual state of arrears) never mind ten large to pay a tramp so that he'll—

'They're going to find out anyway, Liam, Mummy and Daddy. But let's say you don't ask 'em, that you simply can't find the bottle to have that conversation. Here's how that goes. You get arrested, you go to court and, okay, you get to tell your side of the story. Let's call that "the truth". Then Miller gets up, gets to tell his little story. Let's call that one "the facts". Now, the judge ain't interested in the truth, Liam, and you need to remember that. He's only interested in the facts, and my guess is that based on them he'd have no hesitation in putting you away. Imagine that, Mummy crying in the courtroom, Daddy holding her tightly, stone-faced and unable to look at his disgraced son getting dragged from the stand. Brings a tear to my eye, Liam, it really does. But let's suppose that the truth did find a way and that the judge ignores the facts, decides to give a poor little rich boy the benefit of the doubt. Do you really think that the rest of us are going to see it that way? Do you really think that Mum and Dad and your future bosses are going to be able to ignore them facts, believe in you again without a shadow of nagging doubt? No, Liam, they won't, and you know it.'

The beardy, insightful prick leans towards me, holds my stare and spells out clearly the conclusion that I've already arrived at. 'And that's why you are going to go back inside, why you are going to choke down that pride and why you are going to ask for the money, because trust me, Liam, it's the only way that Miller's facts go away.'

A smug smile and a confident nod tell me that he knows he's won.

'Wait here. I'll be back in a couple of minutes.'

22

'Mum, do you mind if I talk to Dad alone for a minute? I need to ask him something.'

Mum's birthday is coming up in a couple of weeks, so this request is greeted with a tap on the nose, a knowing wink and a giggly comment about surprise parties and her fake hatred of them. I wink back, having neither the heart nor the time to remind her that parties are illegal during lockdown, unless, that is, you work for a tent supply company. Once she's left, the screen is empty except for the couch and a cushion.

'Dad, are you going to get in the camera or what? I need to tell yo—'

'I can hear you perfectly well without being seen, Liam. So what's this about then?'

Deep breath.

'Well, look, before I start I need to warn you that it's not good, Dad. It's complicated too, so best if you just listen until I've finished, yeah?'

'On you go.'

Another deep breath and I start my tale. Dad does listen, for about twenty seconds, that is, before he sighs and grunts the first of many 'Jesus, Liam's or 'for Christ's sake, son's. The more I reveal the more he interrupts and as the story gets darker the stronger his reactions become until eventually, he is just about as disappointed and angry as I have ever known him, even more so than back in the day when his army life was being stripped away. Dad's finale is a throaty, 'For fuck's sake, lad!'

'I know, I know, Dad, and you're right, it's a lot of money, but shit, what are my options here, I mean, really?'

'Your option is to face up to the bloody consequences for once in your life, Liam! There's no way me and your mum are going to buy you out of this, son, not a chance. And like you say, as bad as it looks, the truth will out and if what you've told me is what really happened then you've got nothing to worry about, have you, son, so no, Liam, the answer's no.'

And there it is. In this one sentence Dad encapsulates everything that I fear and that the tramp explained so clinically. The truth won't 'will out', at least not when it's buried beneath a pile of evidence, no matter how fabricated that evidence might be, but more telling is Dad's final comment: clumsy, doubting words that hit hard. If that's what really happened, he said, if that's what really happened. What chance do I have of ever putting this behind me if Miller has his day in court?

'Please, Dad, please! Look, I know it sounds soft, but do you know the thing that really gets me? Even if you're right and the judge decides to ignore all the evidence, do you really think that everyone else will? I can't live like that, Dad, walking into rooms full of whispers, catching accusing glances and just knowing that I'm continually getting retried and convicted of being a bleedin' murderer by friends, strangers, colleagues! Imagine that, Dad, living a life where no one ever really accepts the truth about you?'

It's a long shot. A last, desperate plea at heartstrings that even as a gooey-eyed toddler I could never play, and it shouldn't have carried much weight, certainly not ten thousand pounds' worth, but after a silence stretched so long that I click the mute button twice to check my speaker's still working, the couch cushion finally talks.

'It'll be in your bank by morning. Don't tell your mum.'

'That is such a relief, Dad, and I promise, I'll pay you back every penny!'

I don't think Dad would have believed me anyway, but as it happens this is a promise that I won't have to break; the call disconnects before I finish. It doesn't matter, though, nothing does now except sealing the deal and getting that huge, homeless monkey off my back and off my balcony for good. In my rush to do this I catch the leg of the coffee table with my trailing foot, so fully that it drags and jolts it, causes Reggie's medals to slide off and onto the floor.

'Shit!'

And then I remember; this isn't evidence anymore! It's just a few pieces of pressed metal junk, and my relief at this realisation is so uplifting that I'm still laughing to myself as I slide the door open and step out onto the balcony, calling out to the tramp even before I can see him.

'I've got your money! I'll have it in my bank—'

Rushing, still too excited to learn the lesson just given, as I turn the corner my foot catches something for a second time, wraps itself around the flimsy white leg of the plastic table where I take my morning coffee. Being so much lighter than the one in the lounge, rather than resist, this time the table flies away. I dive after it, manage to grab its sharp lip just before it tips, thumb planted firmly on top and fingers gripped beneath, one of which presses down on the switch that I'd taped there days before.

The tramp trap ignites. The ball of lights bundled up in the corner of the fire escape explode in a festive fury that showers the tramp's beard with bright shards of green and blue and orange. No longer my smug-faced nemesis, shocked into Santa's evil twin he grips the handrail: manic eyes jarred wide, lips stretched across filthy green teeth by the electricity which is tingling through him. For a long quivering moment he stays like this, staring back at me in disbelief, until finally he finds the strength to release, flings himself backwards, stumbles but somehow manages to stay on his feet until inevitably his third step misses the top tread of the fire escape completely. Try as they might his feet can't find support and so his fall continues, drags him down the stairs, bangs him hard into and then over the handrail! Less than a second after the bottom of his shoes have slipped from sight there is a soft crunch on the paving below. Other than the jingle jangle of flailing feet slapping metal grate, this is the only sound that's made during the whole episode.

'Oh my god! Liam, are you there? Liam! Liam! Are you okay?'

The silence is broken from above, but what to say to

Chloe, what to say! I need time to get my story straight here because this time I am guilty – well, kind of at least. I mean, it was an accident, admittedly an accident caused by a trap that I'd built to do the exact thing that it just did, but I didn't want to electrocute him now, hell no, not now that he's going to help get Miller off my… Shit, he's my alibi!

I ignore Chloe and dash to the balcony wall, knocking the table again but this time allowing it to hit the floor. I lean over the wall as far as I can. Through the fire escape grating I can see the tramp crumpled on the floor. He isn't moving but his arms and legs all look to be in the right place; no backward-facing joints or twisted feet. I need to get down there and see that he's okay, well enough at least to set Miller straight, even if it is with his dying bre—

'Liam, is that you?'

Hearing me move about has chilled Chloe's voice down a notch from her initial shriek and I realise that she probably thought that it had been me that she'd seen in her peripheral, tumbling from the balcony beneath hers.

'Yes, Chloe, it's me, it's me. Wow! Did you see that? Some bloke just jumped off the fire escape!'

Good, this is good. Agreeing on a set of events that we can both recount independently is definitely good.

'Oh, thank god for that, Liam, for a moment there I thought it was you who'd fallen off your—'

'Jumped, Chloe, jumped. I saw him jump, so let's call it jumped, eh, not fallen.'

'Jumped? Really, d'you think? It looked to me like he fell backwards?'

'Did he, though? I'm pretty sure he jumped. I guess it

would be difficult to be sure what happened from where you are, you know, what with your perspective and that. Especially when someone has a beard too. Hard to tell if it's the back of the head or the face that you're looking at from above, don't you think? So let's agree that he jumped, yeah?'

Chloe remains silent as she thinks about this. It's only when I urge her to answer that she does, true enough in tones that are subdued by reluctance but nevertheless buying into my version of events.

'I suppose so. I'll go phone an ambulance.'

This won't do! I need time. Time to return John's Christmas lights to his grotty grotto. Time to check out the tramp's pockets, perhaps, take the opportunity to see if he's holding back on anything or if he's got something stashed in them that can help prove my innocence and maybe save Dad ten grand.

'Well, don't be too hasty here, Chloe. Let's think about this. We don't want to waste some ambulance bloke's time if the geezer's just winded, yeah? Give me a minute and I'll nip down and see how he is, before we start mithering the emergency services.'

'Winded! Jesus, Liam, the bloke just fell three stories from—'

'Jumped, Chloe! I thought we agreed he jumped! Just give me a minute before phoning anyone. I'll shout back up if he needs an ambulance.'

The clock is ticking to Miller's return, so if she is going to object further, I'll have to deal with it from the fire escape whilst I dismantle the tramp trap. As I open the fire escape door, I do catch the last few words of what must have been quite a detailed and concerned challenge to my do-nothing plan, but having missed most of it, all I can do is make a vague guess at an answer, one that is generic enough to hopefully fit whatever it is that she said.

'I hear you, Chloe, but it won't be long now.'

As I talk, I pick at the tape holding the wire to the handrail. I must have done an excellent job of fixing them because of the three bindings I used I can only find the end of one. That one unwraps easily, but as hard as I try to scratch and coax the start of the remaining two it's no good. No good either to simply tug and break the wire because that will leave evidence and Miller already has plenty of that. I need a knife.

'Is he okay?'

Apparently, through four sections of grating, Chloe can't see where the tramp landed, at least not in detail sufficient to be able to tell if I'm there huddled over him or not.

'Not got there yet, Chloe. Just give me a minute, I forgot my first aid kit.'

Back in the kitchen I scrabble through the top drawer, desperate to see the worn wooden handle of the only sharp knife that me and John own. It isn't there and then I remember how he sometimes uses it for shaving blocks of resin into his reefers. Sure enough, the knife is in his secret stash place. I grab it, dash back out to the fire escape and start slicing. The second section of wire releases easy enough, but as I move on to the third and final piece, the fire-escape door opens. Spinning towards it, knife in hand, Margaret screams. I raise my other hand in a gesture intended to show her that it's okay, but she screams again. A policeman drags her back inside, takes her place in the doorway and adopts a textbook stance: knees slightly bent with both arms extended towards me. His shout is excessively loud given that I'm less than a couple of metres away, but I reckon he is must be just out of cop college applying diligently the lessons learnt there.

'Don't move!'

His left hand is empty and open. Stop right there, it says, drop the knife and don't move. His right hand holds a pepper spray, finger poised to trigger it. Have a go, you little shit, it says, please have a go so I can take you down. I do as the right hand suggests, drop the knife and listen to it jingle jangle on the grate. The sound takes the heat out of the situation, and the copper lowers his arms and straightens up. He is huge and looks disappointed.

'That's a smart decision. Now, do you want to tell me who you are and what you're doing on the fire escape with a knife?'

I use the cover of relaxing my stance to shuffle around a little, stand in front of the final piece of wire that's still taped to the handrail. This is all the delay I can afford; the quicker I answer him the more believable my story will be.

'Liam, Liam Slater. I live here, Officer, apartment three fourteen, just behind you on the right. I was in the kitchen doing some lunch when I heard some shouting. At first I thought it was on my balcony but realised it was coming from the fire escape. Couldn't hear what they were saying but one of 'em sounded very aggressive so I went to take a look and still had the knife. As I got here I saw this big bloke pushing what looked like a homeless guy over the handrail then he just ran off.'

The officer steps out onto the fire escape and looks down. 'Shit! You stay here, don't go anywhere, right?'

With that the copper is bounding down the steps, quickly reaching the final switchback and only then realising his schoolboy error, having left alone a potential knife man with a potential murder weapon and a potentially dead Margaret. Sliding to a dead stop he grabs a rail and spins around, like a cartoon cop, then looks up to scream at me.

'You stay exactly where you are and don't touch anything!'

The rookie PC continues to point as he strides back up toward me, tipping and turning his head to keep me in view so that he can be sure I'm complying with his instruction whilst at the same time panting into the radio mic clipped to his lapel, desperate to raise his colleague who apparently is also knocking on doors and investigating Reggie's death. I smile as I watch his previously commanding composure unravel. Only when he steps onto the final set of stairs does he calm. Beyond and below him I can see why: a police woman dashing out of the apartment entrance and kneeling at the side of the lifeless tramp. He takes a deep breath, exhales then clicks his mic button again.

'PC Johnstone to PC Roberts, Johnstone to Roberts, come back.'

There is a brief, buzzing response but one that's far too distorted by the steel structure surrounding us too be deciphered. Still, it's apparently response enough for the panicked copper to clutch at.

'How is he, Sue? Any signs of stab wounds, over?'

Sue's crackling reply is still impossible to understand and so three times PC Johnstone interrupts, tells her that 'you're breaking up, Sue, say again, over'. Eventually Sue gives up, stands and shouts up from the ground. The 'victim' is unconscious but doesn't appear to have been stabbed, we're told. She also confirms that an ambulance has been dispatched. Time is ticking and I can feel my opportunity to cover my tracks slipping away. I need the policeman to go down and join his colleague, but that's not happening, especially now as he's noticed Chloe peering over her balcony wall.

'And what about you, love? Did you see what happened?'

Very matter-of-factly Chloe repeats what we had agreed about how the tramp had jumped from the third-floor fire-escape landing. As she talks the policeman watches me and as he follows up on Chloe's answer, he watches me.

'And did you see or hear anyone else on the fire escape, Chloe?'

'No. Like I say, I just saw him jump. Isn't that right, Liam, love?'

Love! Now it's my turn to answer questions again.

'So, I'll ask you again. Is there anything you want to tell me about the knife, Mr Slater?'

Why the hell did I make up the mystery murderer?! I could have just said that I thought I'd heard two voices, but that when I got here there was only one, mental homeless bloke shouting at the world he was about to leave. Mind you, given the confusion of the last couple of minutes, maybe it's worth a try reselling this.

'No, there isn't. Like I said, I thought I heard two men arguing and that's why I grabbed the knife, but as Chloe said, turns out it was just one suicidal nutter.'

It takes a moment, but the young policeman seems to accept this. That is, until Margaret chirps up.

'But didn't you say that you saw another man push him off the fire escape and then run away?'

Johnstone's face lights up, but before he can jump in, I fire back, hoping to shut this down before it registers.

'Firstly, Margaret, why the hell are you still here, and secondly, why don't you mind you own bloody business!'

Too late, and the copper latches on to Margaret's vindictive accusation. 'Yeah, that's right! You did say that!'

Excited at having his memory jogged, the policeman seems happy to break his oath to serve and protect, to ignore the fact that I've just verbally and rather aggressively assaulted an old-age pensioner, which suits me just fine because I'm not having it!

'What! Now hang on a minute, you can't rely on that interfering old cow to remember shit!'

The three of us are soon arguing like a girl band and we only stop when an authoritative voice booms across from my balcony.

'Now, now, children, let's all calm down, shall we?'

My throat tightens just in time to stop the bile from my stomach rising into my mouth. My time is up.

It's Miller time now.

23

Across the gap, Miller stands and grins at me. From around the corner behind him a woman appears. She's clad head to toe in a white paper suit, but her hair and make-up are ready for a Friday night out with the girls and so she looks more like something you'd see strutting down a Vivian Westwood Covid catwalk than a scene of crime officer. In front of her she holds two clear plastic bags, high in the air for Miller to inspect.

'Arrows and shoes, sir. Is this all you need from the balcony?'

In those two bags are the items that drive a stake into the heart of my defence. Arrows that should be scattered somewhere over the road but apparently were never fired and so make a nonsense of my statement that Reggie had died accidentally after being hit on the head with a child's toy. Trainers that should still be on the tramp's feet but are now back on my table, treads crammed with dried blood and the only possible conclusion being that it was my feet in them, standing next to Reggie as the life bled out of him.

I look down at the man who has framed me. He remains still and lifeless; the only person who can sort this out is at best comatose and more likely dead. Down the street a siren screams. The ambulance is almost here and it's some relief to know that if there is anything left of my star witness then the people who can save him are on their way.

'Actually, Rebecca, before you move inside, could you take some pictures of this and… oh, that too, and then bag it all up. Mark it as victim #2, would you?'

Miller has moved back towards the corner of the building and as he issues instructions he points firstly, at a thin wire snaking inside the patio door towards a plug socket next to my TV and then, as he walks slowly back towards me, at that same cable running along the wall and through the small black switch that's taped underneath the tumbled table. He finishes his sweep with a dramatic, gameshow host arm swing, full circle that when completed jabs a rock steady finger in my direction. Detective Miller tips and lowers his head, closes one eye and sights the other along his arm.

'And Rebecca, same for that tidgy-widgy piece of wire taped to the handrail over there, if you would, love. You see it?'

She confirms that she does and he relaxes, resumes his grin.

'Oh my, Liam, we have been a busy little murderer whilst I've been away, haven't we?'

'He is not a murderer!'

Miller twists his shoulders around, leans over the balcony wall and looks up. 'Hi there! It's Chloe, isn't it? We spoke earlier. So how do you two know each other then?'

Me and Chloe reply to Miller at the same time but not in unison. We do match perfectly the first two words (we and are) but diverge at the last as I complete the answer with 'neighbours' and she goes for 'in a relationship'.

Miller is loving this and starts grinning again. 'Oooh, awkward. So which is it, Liam? Girlfriend or neighbour? Not being nosey, just making sure I get my notes in order.'

I hate this man, I really do, but I also need him to confirm something before I give my final, make-or-break answer. I mouth the word 'swimmer' and punctuate it with a questioning eyebrow pump. He nods back, tight-lipped, rapid nods with eyes slightly closed to affirm his sincerity. I have no choice but to take him at his original word.

'Girlfriend. Yeah, Chloe's my girlfriend.'

An over-enthusiastic yelp of delight from above sets alarm bells ringing. The girl is far too excited about hearing this, far too keen. Miller leans across the wall as far as he can. He sniggers then whispers, 'But I'd say more your pie-munching, greased-up Channel swimmer type, if you know what I mean.'

Above me I can already hear oversized thumbs squidging away as my new girlfriend updates her Facebook status from 'fat and lonely' to 'cuddly and happy'.

God, I hate this man.

Down below there is better news as an ambulance finally pulls up. Its doors open and medics spill out to gather around the tramp.

'Hey, mister ambulance man! Is he dead?!'

One of the men straightens up, leaving his colleague to do her initial checks. I recognise immediately the face that is turning to answer me. The man scratches his head.

'You know, I'm not too sure. What do you reckon? Cover the face or leave it this time? I just can't seem to get the hang of this dead or alive thing. Tell you what, though, it sure does help knowing that you're here to give your expert advice.'

Frustratingly I am now unable to find out if the tramp is dead or not. No point in repeating my question, just to get a surly 'you tell me, smart arse'.

I turn my attention back to Miller, but he isn't on my balcony anymore, having decided that now is the time to join us on the small, grated platform. It feels really crammed on here now, almost claustrophobic, and a quick headcount tells me why. Along with Miller the SOCO is here, busy lifting prints and bagging wire from the handrail. PC Sue has scaled the stairs too so, including me, that makes a total of six crammed on to the fire escape. It's so tight, in fact, that PC Sue has to squeeze past Johnstone so that she can present a folded piece of cardboard to her boss.

'Sir, I found this in the victim's inside coat pocket.'

I wish they'd all stop referring to that conniving bastard as a victim. I'm the real victim here! Having said that, he has been electrocuted and fallen over thirty feet, so I can't really justify why he shouldn't be given this title, I suppose. I am intrigued by the piece of card, though. Why does it look so familiar? Miller unfolds it to read. As it opens, I see a couple of letters written in bold black felt tip and it's enough for me to remember the rest. It gives me great pleasure to spoil Miller's big reveal.

'Don't shoot! It says don't shoot! Ha! Reggie wrote it, when we were doing the arrow thing, so he could tell me if the wind was too strong. And if that was in the tramp's pocket then that means that the tramp had to have been on Reggie's balcony which means you have to believe my story!'

Disappointingly, Miller doesn't seem the slightest bit fazed by my deduction.

'Couple of things, Sherlock. One, it doesn't say don't shoot. It says please don't shoot me, Liam. Two, so what if it was in his pocket? It could have fallen from the balcony when you shot your first victim and the poor sod could have found it in the bushes when he was rummaging around for cigarette butts or whatever it is that they look for these days. In fact, this message, this plea for mercy, is just as likely to prove motive for victim number two, who probably found it and was threatening to take it to the police. Motive enough to electrify a handrail and fake a suicide, wouldn't you say? No, Liam, trust me. This is bad for you.'

I'm not giving up on this, no way, and now that I can see the words in full it's obvious that there are two sets of handwriting in the message. It's as though Lying Larry had thought about using this as another piece of doctored evidence but decided against the idea when he realised how crap his writing was compared to Reggie's. Definitely not bad for me, this Miller; a junior-school English teacher could spot the difference, never mind a graphologist.

'Aw, come on, Miller! Admit it. He's messed with it! He's obviously written my name, anyone can see that, and the only reason he'd do that is if he was going to mess with me too!'

This time Miller does look put out by what I've said, but his puzzled brow soon relaxes. He looks at the young policewoman who brought it to him and concludes what the piece of card in his hand means to his case, offering it back to her and inviting her to finish his sentence.

'So, this is what we in the trade call…?'

It doesn't take long for her to fill in the blank.

'Nevidence, sir. Is it nevidence?'

'Correct! Indeed it is nevidence. Now, do us a favour and lose it, would you?'

I can't believe what I'm hearing! I can't believe what I'm seeing either: a policewoman cramming into her pocket a piece of card that could help my defence before scuttling away, back down the stairs to bin or burn or whatever it!

'What the hell, Miller! Nevidence? What kind of bullshit is that? Stop her!'

Miller shrugs and then explains. 'Look, Mr Slater, I know you think that what you just saw is somehow illegal, but really, it's a grey area. It's nevidence, see, one of those things that doesn't really prove anything either way. But what it does do is… well, to be frank, it just confuses things, drags things out unnecessarily. Better for us, for you, the taxpayer, for everyone if it was never found, never existed and certainly never brought before a judge. So nevidence it is, and believe me, it's for the best, and before you say it, I know that you're going to mention this to your brief when you get one and you're going to be all "and you'll never guess what the coppers did with a piece of evidence, blah blah blah" and do you know what he's going to do? He's going to stop you mid-sentence, before you piss yourself with excitement and then smile a little and say, "Nevidence, aye?" Trust me, it's a thing, Liam, so deal with it because without a witness other than the accused and three police officers, your brief will be smart enough to know to drop it and move on. You should too.'

Behind the detective I see something that he obviously hasn't, something that is going to make him regret his brazen admission to tampering with my evidence.

'Ha! Jokes on you, Miller. There is a witness! Margaret, tell him what you just heard!'

Since I've known Detective Sergeant Miller, admittedly less than a couple of hours, he has been consistently impressive: confident, commanding and in control, but my snappy response has slapped him hard and there are cracks appearing in that character now, cracks through which I can glimpse an ordinary man who is no longer in charge of the situation and visibly concerned about what will happen next. He's gone too early with his mocking nevidence speech and he knows it; dead eyes unable to hide his regret at not having checked around first to see who is actually in earshot on this crowded sheet of grating. Miller swallows hard as Margaret steps forward, brushes past PC Johnstone and positions herself between me and DS Miller. My neighbour gives me a reassuring smile, I mouth 'thank you' and then she turns to face him.

'Mr Miller, I have to tell you that what you just said was, well, quite frankly, it was impossible for me to hear. These old ears of mine, you see, not what they used to be, so if you wouldn't mind, and I apologise for being a... oh, what's the word, oh yes, being an interfering old cow, but if you wouldn't mind terribly, could you repeat what you just said, please?'

You wouldn't think it possible to hate the back of someone's head, but it is. I'm doing it now. Hating the thin curls of grey that barely hide a disgusting collection of age spots and dandruff, all clinging to a wrinkly loose scalp that I so much want to smash my fist through, happy to add this bitch to the list of people whose blood I have on my hands. Across the top of her stupid, sticky-up crown, Miller sighs. The cracks heal and life returns to his eyes. They lock on to me.

'Liam Slater, I am arresting you on suspicion of aggravated burglary and the murder of Reginald Mullen. You have the right to remain silent. Anything you say can and will be used against you in a court of law. You have the right to an attorney and…'

A thick fog has descended on me. Through it I can barely hear my rights being read, but I do hear myself mumbling that I've understood them. PC Johnstone is clamping my wrists now, behind my back, and whilst I am aware of the two steel rings clicking closed, I can't yet feel the pain which I know they are bringing.

'Liam! Liam! I'll wait for you, Liam, I promise I will!'

Oh, I bet she'll wait. Five years waiting for her bad boy gives her the perfect excuse to sit on her fat arse on a sweat-stained sofa taking comfort from an endless bucket of fried chicken.

'They're all people, Liam, they all deserve a bit of love, and believe me, she is going to look a whole lot better after you've had a few years of B-wing showers.'

Somehow, I doubt it.

24

I'm walking now, being led down a seemingly endless spiral to the ground, and it's only when I reach the bottom that a friendly voice manages to pierce the mist and clear my head.

'Liam! What the hell, mate?'

It's Matt! He knows! I've told him pretty much everything, but before I can call back PC Johnstone butts in.

'Hello, Matthew. And what exactly are you doing round here?'

I can't twist fully enough, but from what I can see, Matt looks suddenly weird: childlike and with none of the arrogant swagger that usually defines him.

'I live here now, PC Johnstone, have done for the last three months or so.'

'And does Mr Stevenson know?'

'He does. He came round with me when I signed the lease, so it's all above board. You can check with him if you like.'

The exchange grabs Miller's interest. He drags me to halt then turns me around so that I'm facing my friend, and when he's certain that my face is in clear view, he barks at Matt.

'And does Stevenson know you're knocking around with the likes of him, does he, eh, sunshine? You two big pals? 'Cos if you are then hanging out with murder suspects is just the kind of thing a parole officer might be interested in, don't you think?'

Matt has never once mentioned that he's on parole. Then again, why would he when we really are only balcony buddies, nothing more? I'm surprised by how unsurprised I am at learning this, though. Matt never struck me as being a bad lad, but I suppose on some level there must have always been a question mark in my mind behind which a shady part of him lurked. This revelation makes his testimony in my defence very unlikely. Not that it would have been particularly compelling anyway, I suppose. After all, when you boil it all down, Matt only knows those things that I've told him about me and the tramp. I reckon he understands this too, has already run the pros and cons, but I can still see his discomfort, obviously struggling with the irreconcilable demands of the bro and penal code.

'Hey, Matt, don't sweat it, mate, really.'

The relief in his voice as he answers Miller is obvious. 'We're just neighbours. Chat on the balcony every now and then, but that's as far as it goes.'

Miller seems to accept this, begins to turn me back around so that he can walk me towards the waiting black Mariah, but I resist.

'Hey, Matt, you couldn't do me a solid, could you? I need you to give my dad a call.'

Bit of a contradiction, I know, that such a casual acquaintance should have my dad's number, but though their motives are at opposite ends of the help-Liam spectrum, both Matt and Miller seem happy to hear what I have to say.

'Tell him… tell him that the thing we talked about an hour ago has got all messed up and that there's no need for him to do what he said he would now. Tell him that I'm sorry for the mess too and whilst I really do appreciate the offer, I realise that, like he said, it's time I faced up.'

Matt nods and moves towards the building entrance. Like me, he thinks the message is complete, but for whatever reason, possibly a creeping realisation that what is happening here is going to change my life, I can't put the lid back on the emotional can of worms that these words to my dad have apparently opened.

'And Matt, tell him I'm sorry for messing his life up too, that I understand if he blames me for having to give up the army, yeah? That bit's important.'

Now I can look at Miller, let him know that I'm ready for the van, but he doesn't seem in any hurry. It's as if he needs to take a moment, touched by what he's just heard.

He calls over to Matt. 'Hey, you couldn't give my dad a message too, could you, kiddo? Tell him that I'm really, really sorry for that time I pretended to be sick, bunked off school and took his Ferrari for a joyride.'

I kick myself for yet again mistaking Miller for a decent human being.

'You mean, tell him that you're Ferris Bueller. You're an idiot.'

As mild as it is, my insult earns me a sharp tug and a tightening click of the cuffs.

'Aw, don't be like that, Liam! I thought that's what we

were doing here, being little drama queens. Sue, you got a message for Daddy?'

PC Sue takes her hand from the handle of the van door that she is holding open and grasps her chin in an exaggerated thinking pose.

'Oh yes! Tell my dad that I'm really sorry, but it wasn't those pesky ruffians who stole the pie from the windowsill: it was me.'

Not funny, this, devoid of wit, and Miller's over-enthusiastic laughter gives me the feeling that their relationship is perhaps more than professional, something I should have picked up on earlier, to be honest, when she had been so keen to get behind Miller's nevidence debacle.

Next, it's Johnstone's turn to mock, but being further away and less engaged, when Miller invites him to answer the question his sincere response gets him only tuts and muttered expletives.

'Oh, could you tell my dad to order the pizza for around seven? I'm going to be late tonight.'

Fun over, it's back to the business at hand. Miller shoves me the final few yards, gives me a glimpse of compassion when he warns me to mind my head as I mount the steps to climb into the Mariah, but that soon evaporates. Once hunched through the door frame he pushes hard on my back, causing me to stumble and almost fall into PC Sue, who is sat waiting for me to join her on the narrow bench seat.

'Be back in five. Just going to have a quick chat with the medics. Now don't you be naughty while I'm gone.'

Miller winks as he closes the door. I'm tempted to flip him a finger but stop before I do, suddenly aware of a horribly disturbing truth. Those words, that wink, they weren't meant for me, they were to remind his lover of some dirty, handcuffed session in this very van, and the image of Miller's naked arse squidging around where I'm sat tortures me as I await my fate in the gloomy silence.

25

I can't be sure how long I've been sat here replaying Miller's bouncing buttocks, but finally my torment is ended, interrupted by a loud ruckus kicking off outside. Initially two then three voices, each not quite shouting but all raised, demanding to be heard above the others and occasionally aggressive.

'Stay put!'

PC Sue's order has an unexpected and undeniable authority to it, this eager-to-please underling invoking a confident, professional poise as she readies herself to deal with whatever situation is developing outside. Her left hand reaches for the door handle whilst at the same time her right releases a slim black baton holstered to her thigh. One final warning look back as she drops out of the van doesn't need words, but what she fails to do, in her haste to join the fray, is properly latch the van closed. PC Sue didn't say anything about me not looking, so I push the door wide open with my foot.

Framed by the dark Mariah, the scene I'm watching play out is full of contradictions. For a start, PC Johnstone is no longer the submissive beat cop to Miller's tough-talking, renegade detective. Now he's the principled young policeman, doing whatever he must in order to honour the badge, even if his actions might mean having to hand it over tomorrow. Johnstone is restraining Miller! He has his boss's arms twisted high up his back to prevent Miller from doing whatever it is that he would if he were freed. The detective has lost it, shouting over and over that, 'He's my fuckin' witness, dickhead!' PC Sue arrives, intervenes and pulls to one side a very agitated medic, herself bawling back into Miller's face. 'And I'm telling you he's my patient!' she insists. As the pair are pulled apart, I get to see into the back of the ambulance.

And there he is, amongst the bottles and masks and machines that go ping: Lying Larry Smith sat upright on an orange gurney! Lying Lazarus Smith, back from the dead! But as shocking as this sight is, it's nothing compared to the mind-bending figure who's sat next to him.

It's a woman. A familiar woman wearing a dress that I've admired once before. A woman with soft, shoulder-length hair that I also recognise, from Dad's shed. A woman who looks disturbingly like the older sister I never had.

'Dad?'

It bloody is him! It's my dad, sat next to my nemesis, wearing women's clothes and chatting away through a huge, lipstick grin.

'Sod you, PC Sue.'

Miller is the first to see me climb out of the black Mariah and jog over towards the crowd.

'Hey! Get back in the bloody van, you!'

PC Johnstone is still holding his boss firm, and as the medic hasn't yet calmed either, all three coppers have their hands full, so my route to the ambulance is unimpeded. Once there, stood looking in, no one about me seems too concerned. It's as if the whole world has turned again whilst I'd been locked in the dark.

'Dad, what the hell are you wearing?'

Dad glances in my direction, but only momentarily. Totally unflustered, calmly and purposefully, he turns back to the tramp, takes that beardy face in his huge hands and tips it up slightly so that their stares lock.

'So, we understand each other then.'

The tramp nods.

'Good.'

Only now does my dad look at me. He stands, as best he can in the cramped space, then brushes down the creases from his satin dress before finally answering, 'Michael Kors, son. Why, what are you wearing?'

There should be questions, hundreds of them, but there aren't, at least none that I don't already know the answer to. Shit, I've wasted enough hangover mornings in front of daytime TV to know why my dad is dressed like this. I know too how hard it must be for him to reveal the true Billy Slater and that it isn't relief that's put a confident smile on his face; it's pride. Yeah, I get it completely, because I'm proud of him too. Rather awkwardly he clambers down from the ambulance, legs too wide and skirt riding high. After a necessary adjustment to protect his modesty Dad adopts a more feminine pose: hands on his waist, knees together and hips turned slightly towards me.

'So, what do you reckon?'

'I reckon you need to lose the trainers, Dad. They make your outfit look tacky.'

He relaxes his stance, hands dropping, flapping at his side as if he isn't sure what to do with them, having no pockets and all. I feel bad, as though what I said has made him feel conscious of his look, his choice of footwear.

'Yeah. I was in a bit of a hurry after Matt called. Bit confused too, to be honest. I got that you needed help, but what was all that about a Ferrari and a pie?'

Behind him PC Sue and the medic have climbed in beside the stretcher to sit either side of the tramp. The medic is taking his blood pressure; the policewoman is taking notes. I nod in their direction.

'What did you say to him?'

Dad looks back over his shoulder pads, gives the tramp a thumbs-up and then looks back at me to explain. 'I just asked him who he was, Liam. Turns out that Danny used to be in the Lancaster Brigade, deployed in Iraq just after I finished my tour there. Didn't handle it too well, though, got discharged with PTSD. Poor sod's been on the street ever since. Sad, really, but I convinced him to tell the police what's really gone on.'

Dad reaches out, and his firm grip on my elbow feels good, although I must admit that those perfectly painted red nails do look a bit strange.

'It's all sorted, son.'

And now I do have a question for him. One that's been bugging me for nearly twenty years.

'Dad, do you still blame me for your army career ending like it did?'

As he lets go of my arm, Dad takes a step back. The reassuring smile is replaced by a stern scowl, as if he's disappointed that I could even think something like this.

'Yeah, I meant to ask you about that. Matt mentioned you saying sorry, me blaming you for screwing up my life or something like that. What the hell was that about?'

'Well, maybe blame is too strong a word. Resent, perhaps? Did you resent me being born and you and Mum having to leave Germany?'

I've ran through this a thousand times. Sometimes Dad shouts back that yes, I ruined his life; other times he breaks down, admits that he hated me. In not one of those scenarios does he deliver a cursory, blunt dismissal of my quandary.

'I'll say this and only this, Liam. Your mum's always had my back, even with everything I've put her through. She's my rock and it was her who decided when it was time for me to leave the army. It was nothing to do with you then and it's nothing to do with you now.'

Initially disappointing, on reflection, Dad's dismissive attitude is comfortably reassuring because despite the glamorous garb, he's still the same hardnosed, no-nonsense pain in the arse that he always has been.

'Hey, Liam!'

The tramp's shout is a welcome distraction, giving me an out from what was in danger of becoming a bit of a standoff moment with the potential to blow up into a barny.

'Yeah?'

'I was just telling this police lady about the trainers. You know, the ones that you gave me and then I tried to use them to set you up? She was saying that you said that they were yours, but you gave them to me, right? Or am I not remembering things clearly?'

Bastard has finally got my trainers! Jesus, is this what all this has been about? Really? A pair of bloody shoes!

'No, you're remembering just fine. I gave them to you, Danny. They're all yours.'

Danny nudges PC Sue, making sure that she's writing all this down, and only when he's certain that the transfer of ownership of my trainers has been recorded as part of an official statement does he look at me again. Something is different about his face, though; it's softer somehow, less of a rage-against-the-world grimace behind his eyes. Maybe this wasn't about the shoes after all. Maybe it was all just about his name, about me knowing and using it. About him being acknowledged.

And then he speaks again.

'Oh, good. I knew I was right because that was the same time that you said that you'd like to give me your laptop. Remember, I saw it through the window, commented on what a good model it was? Or am I getting my facts confused again?'

Nope, nothing to do with him hearing his name then; Danny is a conniving, robbing knobhead. But two can play at this game.

'You know, Danny, I think you are right. But remember, then you said that whilst it was a very generous offer, there'd be little point in you taking it because you had nowhere to charge it up. Write that down too, if you don't mind, please.'

'Yes, I did say that! Now I remember, but then you insisted, said that I should have it anyway and that I could come and charge it up in your place anytime I liked.'

And now he has my laptop. I need to shut up before I lose my TV, but I also need to check with Dad, see how solid he thinks that Lying Larry Smith's promise to clear my name is, now that he's witnessed first-hand this tricky bastard at his best.

'Can we trust him, Dad?'

Dad sighs. 'It's simple, son. You have no choice. Look, Danny's a survivor, an opportunist, but he's also a realist. He knows that he's had just about all the fun he's going to get out of you. And don't confuse the two either, because although he likes to mess with people, that doesn't mean that he hasn't got pride in the man he was for most of his life. He isn't going to risk losing that so yes, I think we can trust him. Unless, that is, you want to take a risk and try and get your stuff back, but the way I see it, you've lost, son. Best to accept that and move on, eh?'

I'm about to answer, but PC Sue is here. She's turning me around as she interrupts. 'Sorry to butt in like this, gentlemen, or is it ladies and, oh, I am so sorry but how do you—'

'Gentlemen is fine, love. Please, don't feel awkward.'

PC Sue blushes. 'Anyway, let's get these cuffs off, shall we? I've got everything I need, and on behalf of the arresting officer I can only apologise for the misunderstanding and—'

'Sue! What are you doing? Put those cuffs back on my suspect now, and that's an order!'

PC Johnstone is still holding Miller, but as his captive had calmed considerably, it is no longer with that textbook restraining arm twist. The detective sergeant breaks away with little effort, storms towards us. I can feel the young policewoman's hands trembling, fumbling with the cuff key behind my back.

'PC Roberts, stop! You do not release my murder suspect based on whatever that lowlife tramp said, especially since he's been got to by this, this, whatever this hairy, fucked-up perverted freak is!'

They say that you can take the man out of the army, but you can never take the army out of the man, even if that man is now wearing mascara and blusher. With controlled speed and powerful precision my dad drops his shoulder, spreads his stance and punches a solid blow into Miller's belly. Miller heaves, crunches over, struggling to get his shocked diaphragm pulling air again. Like this he wheezes a second order, this time to Johnstone.

'Nick him! That's ABH, that is!'

My arms have finally been freed and so it's PC Sue who is the first to react. She comes around me, stands in front of my dad, and the pair exchange a look. Satisfied by whatever it is that she saw behind those fluttering lashes, PC Sue spins around to face Miller.

'Didn't look like ABH to me, sir, more like KBH. Remember that? I think you introduced me to the idea around the same time as nevidence. Karmic Bodily Harm, you called it. That thing you like to dish out when someone does something that isn't worth wasting the duty sergeant's ink but deserves a good slap anyway? Well, sir, consider yourself slapped.'

Case closed, PC Sue points away from the ambulance and urges us to go, quickly too. Me and Dad take her advice and leave the scene, walk off quickly, in no particular direction. We don't talk, we don't stop our brisk stroll until we reach the small park gate opposite the bench where the bearded, homeless soldier who started all this once sat. Left or right are the options. There's no going back.

'So, what do you fancy doing? Cup of tea with your mum? She is going to be so made up that this is all out in the open, I can tell you.'

I do want this, to sit and chat, but there's something else that I want to do first.

'Yeah, but let's take the path on the right, take the long way round. I want to see if Granddad is up and about.'

Dad likes the idea. 'Good call. I tell you what, though, this is really going to mess with the old fella's head! Hey, a tenner says that he thinks I'm your mum.'

I take his hand and shake it to accept the bet.

'Tenner says he thinks you're Susan Boyle.'